THE KILLER NEXT DOOR

The Ordinary Faces of Murder

K. ELEANOR

"You never really know a man until you stand in his shoes and walk around in them."

— *Harper Lee, To Kill a Mockingbird*

Contents

Introduction

5 - The Masks We Wear

Chapter 1 – Ted Bundy

8 - The Charmer Who Hid a Monster

10 - Early Life: Shaping the Mask

13 - The Charismatic Killer Emerges

19 - The Crimes: A Pattern of Deception and Horror

25 - The Trial: A Charmer in Court

31 - Psychological Analysis: The Mind Behind the Mask

38 - Legacy: Lessons from the Boy Next Door

Chapter 2 – John Wayne Gacy

45 - The Clown with a Dark Secret: John Wayne Gacy

47 - Early Life and Troubled Foundations

50 - The Double Life Begins

54 - Pogo the Clown and the Perfect Façade

58 - The Killing Spree

62 - The Investigation and Capture

67 - The Trial and Media Frenzy

71 - Prison Years and Legacy

Chapter 3 – Dennis Rader, BTK

76 - BTK – The Hidden Face of Evil

77 - Early Life and Formative Years

82 - The Making of a Double Life

88 - The Birth of BTK

93 - Taunting the Police and Media

98 - The Continued Killing Spree

103 - The BTK Hiatus

108 - Resurfacing and Capture

112 - Confession and Trial
117 - Legacy and Lessons: Understanding the Impact of BTK

Chapter 4 – Nannie Doss:

123 – Nanny Doss: 'The Giggling Granny'
129 - Early Marriages on the Path to Darkness
134 - The Lonely Hearts Killer: A Pattern Emerges
139 - Family Ties and Betrayal: Killing Those Closest
144 - The Downfall: Samuel Doss and the End of a Killing Spree
149 - The Giggling Confession
159 - Legacy of a Killer: Lessons from Nanny Doss

164 – Deception in the Shadows
169 - The Manipulative Spouse: Love as a Weapon
176 - The Fraudulent Friend: Betrayal in Close Circles
183 - The Double Life: Ordinary Faces, Extraordinary Secrets
190 – Professional Deceivers: Con Artists and Fraudsters
197 - Psychological Manipulators: Cult Leaders and Charismatic Liars
203 – Overlooked Justice: Why Deceptive Crimes are Often Missed
211 - Lessons from the Shadows: Protecting Against Deception

The Masks We Wear

Appearances have always been the foundation of trust. We rely on first impressions, the warmth of a smile, the friendliness of a wave, and the ordinariness of the people around us to assure ourselves that the world is safe. Yet, what happens when that trust is misplaced? What happens when the friendly neighbour, the helpful coworker, or even the respected community leader is not who they seem to be?

History is littered with stories that challenge our instincts and shatter our illusions of security. These are the stories of individuals who, to all outward appearances, were ordinary—some even charming or admirable. But behind the mask of normalcy, they harboured darkness. They lived double lives, presenting one version of themselves to the world while committing acts of unimaginable horror in the shadows.

The idea of the "killer next door" is chilling precisely because it feels so personal. These are not shadowy figures skulking in alleys or faraway criminals whose lives seem distant from our own. These are the people we know—or think we know. They are the man who fixes your car, the woman who smiles at your children in the park, the church leader who guides your community, or the friendly neighbour who brings over a plate of cookies.

In this book, we will examine the lives of some of the most infamous individuals who fit this unsettling profile. People like Ted Bundy, whose charm and intelligence masked a terrifying predatory nature; John Wayne Gacy, a respected businessman and children's entertainer who hid a horrific secret; and Dennis Rader, the family man and church president who turned out to be the BTK killer. We will also uncover the lesser-known stories of individuals who used their unassuming demeanour as a weapon, slipping under society's radar for years.

But this book is not just about the killers. It's about us—about the societal blind spots, cultural norms, and ingrained assumptions that allowed these individuals to hide in plain sight. Why are we so quick to trust appearances? Why do we ignore red flags, even when they're waving in front of us? And what does it say about human nature that we often fail to recognise evil when it wears a friendly face?

As we delve into these stories, we'll confront uncomfortable truths about the fragility of trust and the ease with which deception can thrive. Each chapter will peel back the layers of the masks these killers wore, examining not only their crimes but also the mechanisms that allowed them to remain undetected for so long.

The purpose of this book is not to frighten but to illuminate. By understanding the lives and behaviours of those who hid their darkness so well, we can better protect ourselves and our communities. Evil, as we will see, often looks nothing like we expect. It's not always the stranger lurking in the dark; sometimes, it's the person holding the door open for you or inviting you over for coffee.

So, let us begin this unsettling journey into the lives of those who proved that appearances can indeed be deceiving. This is not just a collection of stories about killers—it's a study of the masks we all wear and a reminder that sometimes, the most ordinary faces can conceal the most extraordinary horrors.
.

1
Ted Bundy – The Charmer Who Hid a Monster

Ted Bundy was the quintessential "boy next door." Handsome, intelligent, and outwardly charismatic, he embodied the kind of person parents hoped their daughters would bring home. With his clean-cut appearance and air of ambition, Bundy seamlessly blended into society, disarming those around him with his charm. But beneath the surface lay a predator whose heinous crimes shocked the world and shattered the illusion of safety for a generation.

Bundy's ability to hide his depravity behind a façade of normalcy is what makes his story so chilling. He wasn't the shadowy figure lurking in dark alleys; he was the man who held the door open for strangers, volunteered at a crisis hotline, and studied law to "make a difference." His double life exposed a terrifying truth: evil doesn't always look evil.

This chapter delves into the life of Ted Bundy—the calculated manipulator who used his charm as a weapon. From his seemingly ordinary beginnings to his horrifying reign of terror, Bundy's story forces us to question how well we truly know those around us. How did he cultivate the trust of his victims? Why did so many ignore the red flags? And how did one man exploit society's blind spots to become one of history's most infamous serial killers?

As we unravel Bundy's life, we'll explore the interplay between his outward persona and inner darkness, peeling back the layers of a man who was, in every sense, the killer next door.

Early Life: Shaping the Mask

Ted Bundy was born on November 24, 1946, at the Elizabeth Lund Home for Unwed Mothers in Burlington, Vermont. His mother, Louise Cowell, was 22 years old, unmarried, and facing the societal stigma of raising a child out of wedlock. To protect her from shame, her parents decided to raise Ted as their own child, leading him to believe that his mother was actually his older sister. This early deception set the stage for Bundy's later struggles with identity and emotional detachment. The identity of his father remains uncertain, with Louise offering conflicting stories over the years. Some accounts suggest he was an Air Force veteran who abandoned her, while others point to more sinister possibilities, including family rumours that Louise's own father, Samuel Cowell, might have been involved. Though there is no evidence to substantiate these darker theories, the ambiguity surrounding Bundy's parentage created a murky foundation that likely influenced his perception of himself and the world.

Bundy's early years in the Cowell household were far from nurturing. His grandfather, Samuel, was a domineering and volatile figure, described by family members as abusive and unrelenting. Samuel had a notorious temper, physically disciplining both pets and children, and showing little tolerance for disobedience. His bigoted and controlling nature created an oppressive environment, while Bundy's grandmother, Eleanor, provided little reprieve. Timid and emotionally fragile, Eleanor suffered from severe depression and agoraphobia, often retreating into silence. She reportedly underwent electroconvulsive therapy for her condition, leaving Bundy without a stable maternal figure during his formative years. While Bundy would later deny experiencing abuse in his childhood, it's clear that his home life was fraught with tension and emotional instability. Family members also recalled early signs of Bundy's peculiar behaviour, such as his fascination with knives and tendency to isolate himself. While these behaviours were largely dismissed at the time as quirks of a shy and awkward boy, they foreshadowed the darkness that would later surface.

In 1950, when Bundy was just four years old, Louise moved with him across the country to Tacoma, Washington. There, she sought a fresh start and eventually married Johnny Bundy, a hospital cook who adopted Ted as his own son. Despite Johnny's efforts to provide a stable and loving environment, Ted harboured disdain for his stepfather, whom he viewed as unremarkable and unworthy of respect. This sense of superiority, even as a child, was one of Bundy's defining traits. While Johnny worked hard to provide for the family and included Ted in camping trips and other bonding activities, Ted dismissed him, feeling that he did not measure up to the ambitions and self-image Ted was beginning to cultivate. This growing sense of entitlement would later become a defining characteristic, as Bundy believed himself to be above others, deserving of whatever he desired, no matter the consequences.

Throughout his school years, Bundy's life was marked by a mix of academic success and social isolation. On the surface, he was intelligent, achieving good grades and excelling in subjects that piqued his interest. Teachers often saw him as a bright and capable student. However, his peers remembered a different side of Bundy—someone who struggled to form close friendships and often seemed out of place. He described himself as a loner, someone who felt invisible to those around him. This duality—of outward competence and inner alienation—began to shape the mask Bundy would later wear. Even as a teenager, he started to craft a charming and confident persona that masked his insecurities. By high school, Bundy had learned how to win the favour of teachers and classmates when it suited him, but these connections were often shallow and calculated.

Ted's childhood and adolescence were a study in contrasts. Behind the polite, well-behaved boy was someone increasingly aware of his ability to manipulate others. His growing self-perception as smarter and more deserving than those around him clashed with a deep-seated insecurity about his place in the world. These conflicting feelings—the need to belong and the need to dominate—would continue to grow, shaping the man who would one day become one of the most infamous serial killers in history. As he moved through his teenage years and into adulthood, Bundy's ability to mask his true self became not only a skill but a weapon, one that allowed him to hide his predatory nature behind a façade of charm and normalcy. The boy who was once dismissed as awkward and peculiar would become a master of deception, a manipulator capable of disarming even the most cautious individuals. His early life, while outwardly unremarkable, laid the foundation for the mask that would conceal a monster.

The Charismatic Killer Emerges

Ted Bundy's transition from a socially awkward teenager to a calculated predator was not abrupt but rather a gradual evolution rooted in his ability to craft a convincing mask of charm and normalcy. By the time he entered adulthood, Bundy had learned to manipulate those around him, presenting himself as someone who was not only trustworthy but also magnetic. His confidence, intelligence, and seemingly warm demeanour disarmed many, allowing him to gain access to victims who might otherwise have been wary. It was this calculated combination of traits—his charm, intellect, and cold-blooded nature—that would allow him to evade capture for years and commit some of the most infamous crimes in American history.

In the late 1960s, Bundy attended the University of Puget Sound before transferring to the University of Washington to study Chinese. It was during this time that he met Stephanie Brooks, a woman who would leave a profound impact on him. Stephanie was everything Bundy aspired to be: attractive, educated, and from a wealthy, respected family. For a time, their relationship appeared promising, but Stephanie ultimately ended things, citing Bundy's lack of direction and ambition. This rejection devastated him, but it also lit a fire within him. Determined to prove her wrong and win her back, Bundy worked to transform himself into the kind of man he believed she would value. He began dressing more sharply, cultivating a polished, professional image, and even re-enrolled at the University of Washington to study psychology, where he excelled academically.

Bundy's efforts to reinvent himself went beyond superficial changes. He sought out roles and opportunities that would bolster his image as a compassionate and driven individual. One of the most notable examples of this was his work at a suicide prevention hotline. This position, which seemed to showcase Bundy's empathy and desire to help others, allowed him to forge close relationships with his coworkers, including future true crime writer Ann Rule. Rule, who would later write the seminal book *The Stranger Beside Me* about her experiences with Bundy, described him as kind, attentive, and genuinely interested in helping people in crisis. The irony of Bundy's role at the hotline—a man saving lives while secretly harbouring a desire to take them—illustrates the depth of his duplicity.

By the early 1970s, Bundy was deeply embedded in the Seattle social scene. He became active in local politics, working on the campaign of Republican governor candidate Daniel J. Evans. Bundy's intelligence, charisma, and ability to connect with people made him a valuable asset to the campaign. At the same time, he began dating another woman, Elizabeth Kloepfer, a single mother who would later play a pivotal role in his eventual capture. Elizabeth described Bundy as attentive and loving, though their relationship was marred by his frequent disappearances and erratic behaviour. To her, Bundy was the perfect boyfriend—charming, caring, and eager to step into a fatherly role for her daughter. Yet, even as he cultivated this image of a devoted partner, Bundy was already plotting the crimes that would eventually expose his true nature.

Bundy's ability to compartmentalise his life was key to his success as a predator. He maintained the façade of an ambitious, caring man while secretly honing his methods of manipulation and control. He began to target young women, carefully observing their behaviours and vulnerabilities. Bundy understood that societal expectations often made women more likely to trust a well-dressed, articulate man who appeared to need help. He exploited these dynamics to devastating effect, often using ruses to lure his victims. One of his most common tactics involved pretending to have an injury or disability. Bundy would wear a sling or a cast, approach women in public places, and ask for their assistance with seemingly innocuous tasks, such as loading books into his car. Once the women were close enough, he would overpower them, bind them, and transport them to secluded locations.

The 1974 disappearance of several young women in the Pacific Northwest marked the beginning of Bundy's reign of terror. Each victim fit a specific profile: white, slender, with long dark hair parted in the middle. This resemblance was not coincidental; many believed Bundy's victims bore a striking similarity to Stephanie Brooks, his former girlfriend whose rejection had left such a lasting impact. It was as though Bundy was attempting to recreate and control the narrative of his own heartbreak, exacting revenge on women who symbolised what he could not have.

One of the most chilling aspects of Bundy's crimes was the ease with which he blended into his surroundings. In July 1974, he approached Janice Ott and Denise Naslund on the same day at Lake Sammamish State Park, using the same ruse—a fake injury and a request for help carrying his belongings to his car. Despite the park being crowded with families and groups of friends, Bundy managed to lure both women to their deaths without arousing suspicion. Witnesses later described him as "handsome" and "clean-cut," a man who didn't fit the stereotype of a dangerous predator. This ability to appear so ordinary, even charming, was Bundy's greatest weapon.

As Bundy's confidence grew, so did the boldness of his crimes. He began travelling to other states, including Utah, Colorado, and Idaho, to avoid detection. His pattern of abducting, assaulting, and killing young women remained consistent, but his methods became increasingly violent. Bundy was not content with simply taking lives; he derived pleasure from the suffering of his victims, often returning to the sites of their bodies to engage in necrophilic acts. This escalation in brutality reflected not only his sadistic tendencies but also his growing sense of invincibility.

Despite the mounting number of disappearances, law enforcement agencies were slow to connect the dots. At the time, communication between jurisdictions was limited, and the idea of a single individual being responsible for such widespread carnage was almost unthinkable. Bundy's ability to evade capture was further aided by his intelligence and adaptability. When police in Utah finally arrested him in 1975 for possession of burglary tools, Bundy remained calm and cooperative, denying any involvement in the disappearances. Even when evidence began to mount against him, Bundy's charm and confidence made it difficult for investigators to reconcile the image of the polite, well-educated man in front of them with the horrific crimes they were investigating.

As Bundy's crimes continued to make headlines, a composite sketch of the suspected perpetrator was widely circulated. The sketch, based on eyewitness accounts, bore a striking resemblance to Bundy, and several people, including Elizabeth Kloepfer, contacted authorities to report their suspicions. However, Bundy's outward normalcy and lack of a criminal record led many to dismiss these tips. Kloepfer, who was deeply conflicted about her suspicions, remained in a relationship with Bundy even as she provided information to the police. Her reluctance to believe that the man she loved could be a killer highlights the power of Bundy's manipulative charm.

Bundy's arrest in Utah marked the beginning of his downfall, but even in custody, he continued to use his charisma to manipulate those around him. During interrogations, he maintained his innocence, often charming investigators and sowing doubt about his involvement. His intelligence and legal knowledge allowed him to navigate the judicial system with ease, delaying his trials and confounding prosecutors. When faced with evidence he couldn't refute, Bundy would pivot, using his wit and charisma to deflect attention from his crimes.

By the time Bundy's true nature was fully revealed, the scope of his crimes had left an indelible mark on American society. His ability to hide in plain sight, leveraging his charm and intelligence to gain trust, shattered the illusion that evil could always be recognised. Bundy's story serves as a chilling reminder that danger does not always wear the face of a monster; sometimes, it looks like the boy next door. The charismatic killer had emerged, leaving behind a trail of devastation that would haunt the nation for decades to come.

The Crimes: A Pattern of Deception and Horror

Ted Bundy's reign of terror officially began in 1974, though many experts believe his first murder occurred years earlier. His methods were as chilling as they were calculated, relying on a combination of charm, cunning, and meticulous planning to lure unsuspecting victims into his trap. For Bundy, the act of killing wasn't just about the physical violence—it was about power, control, and the thrill of deception. He thrived on outsmarting those around him, whether they were his victims, law enforcement, or the public at large. His crimes spanned multiple states and claimed the lives of at least 30 women, though the true number remains unknown. Each crime bore Bundy's signature: a carefully crafted ruse, a brutal attack, and a sinister pattern of post-mortem behaviour that showcased the depth of his depravity.

Bundy's victims were almost exclusively young women, typically in their late teens or early twenties, with long dark hair parted down the middle. This physical profile was not coincidental; it bore a striking resemblance to Stephanie Brooks, the woman who had rejected him during his college years. Many psychologists have speculated that Bundy's murders were, in part, an attempt to exact revenge on women who symbolised his former girlfriend, projecting his anger and feelings of inadequacy onto his victims. However, Bundy's crimes went beyond a simple psychological fixation—they were acts of calculated cruelty, designed to inflict maximum terror and exert complete control.

Bundy's methods were chillingly effective. He would often approach women in public places, such as college campuses, parks, or shopping malls, using a carefully rehearsed ruse to gain their trust. One of his most infamous tactics involved feigning injury or disability. Bundy would wear a sling or cast on his arm or leg and carry a set of crutches, creating the appearance of vulnerability. He would then ask his intended victim for help with a seemingly harmless task, such as carrying books to his car or loading a sailboat onto a trailer. Once the woman agreed to assist him, Bundy would strike, overpowering her with terrifying efficiency. His ability to appear so unthreatening, combined with his good looks and charming demeanour, made him an incredibly effective predator. Time and again, his victims were disarmed by his outward normalcy, never suspecting the danger that awaited them.

The year 1974 marked a turning point in Bundy's criminal career, as he embarked on a killing spree that would span several states. His first known attacks occurred in Washington state, where he targeted women at the University of Washington and nearby areas. On January 4, 1974, Bundy broke into the basement apartment of 18-year-old Karen Sparks, a student at the University of Washington. He bludgeoned her with a metal rod and sexually assaulted her, leaving her for dead. Miraculously, Sparks survived, but the attack left her with permanent physical and psychological damage. This assault marked the beginning of Bundy's escalating violence, as he grew increasingly confident in his ability to evade detection.

Over the following months, Bundy's crimes became more frequent and more brazen. In February 1974, he abducted and killed Lynda Ann Healy, another University of Washington student. Healy, like many of Bundy's victims, was a bright and ambitious young woman with a promising future. Bundy broke into her room late at night, subdued her, and carried her away while her roommates slept just a few feet away. Her disappearance was initially treated as a missing person case, but it would later become clear that Healy had fallen victim to a serial predator.

As the months went on, Bundy's confidence grew, and so did his willingness to take risks. He began targeting women in broad daylight, often in crowded public places where witnesses were plentiful. One of the most infamous examples of this occurred on July 14, 1974, at Lake Sammamish State Park in Washington. Bundy approached several women at the park, introducing himself as "Ted" and claiming he needed help loading a sailboat onto his car. Witnesses later recalled seeing a handsome, well-dressed man wearing a sling, speaking politely and exuding confidence. Two women, Janice Ott and Denise Naslund, agreed to help him—and neither was ever seen alive again. Bundy's audacity in abducting two women on the same day from such a crowded location underscored his growing sense of invincibility.

Despite the growing number of disappearances, law enforcement agencies struggled to identify a suspect. At the time, the concept of a serial killer—a single individual committing multiple murders across different jurisdictions—was not well understood, and communication between police departments was limited. Bundy exploited these gaps in the system, moving from state to state to avoid detection. After exhausting opportunities in Washington, he relocated to Utah in the fall of 1974, where he enrolled in law school at the University of Utah. But his academic pursuits were merely a cover for his continued predatory behaviour. In October of that year, Bundy abducted and murdered Melissa Smith, the 17-year-old daughter of a local police chief, followed by 17-year-old Laura Aime just weeks later. Both victims were subjected to horrific violence, including strangulation and post-mortem sexual assault.

Bundy's crimes in Utah bore the same hallmarks as his earlier murders: a well-rehearsed ruse, a carefully selected victim, and an almost clinical attention to detail in disposing of the bodies. Yet, despite his meticulous planning, Bundy's growing arrogance began to leave him vulnerable. On November 8, 1974, Bundy approached Carol DaRonch at a shopping mall in Murray, Utah, posing as a police officer. He claimed her car had been broken into and asked her to accompany him to the station. Suspicious but compliant, DaRonch agreed, only to realise something was wrong when Bundy attempted to handcuff her. She managed to escape, providing police with a detailed description of her attacker. This close call marked one of the first cracks in Bundy's carefully constructed façade, but it would still be months before he was apprehended.

Bundy's crimes escalated further in 1975, as he expanded his hunting grounds to include Colorado. His pattern remained consistent: young women, often students, abducted and murdered in remote locations. One of the most harrowing cases from this period involved Caryn Campbell, a 23-year-old nurse who disappeared from a ski resort in Aspen. Her body was discovered weeks later, discarded in the wilderness, bearing the same signs of violence that had characterised Bundy's earlier victims. The randomness of his attacks and the vast geographic area he covered made it nearly impossible for law enforcement to connect the dots, allowing Bundy to continue his killing spree unchecked.

What set Bundy apart from other killers was not just the sheer number of his victims but the calculated nature of his crimes. He meticulously planned each abduction, studying his victims and the locations where he would strike. He often scouted potential targets for days or even weeks, observing their routines and looking for vulnerabilities. His ability to blend in and appear completely unremarkable was one of his greatest weapons. Witnesses frequently described him as "normal," "polite," and "attractive," traits that made it difficult for anyone to suspect him of such heinous acts. Even those who interacted with Bundy on a personal level—friends, coworkers, and romantic partners—had no inkling of his true nature.

Bundy's methods were not only brutal but also deeply personal. He often spent hours with his victims, subjecting them to prolonged suffering before finally killing them. Afterward, he would return to the sites where he had disposed of their bodies, sometimes days or weeks later, to engage in necrophilic acts. This behaviour underscored Bundy's need for control and dominance, as well as his complete lack of empathy. For Bundy, the act of killing was not just about ending a life—it was about asserting his power and reducing his victims to objects that he could manipulate at will.

By the time Bundy was finally arrested in August 1975, the scope of his crimes was beginning to come into focus, though the full extent would not be understood for years. His ability to deceive, manipulate, and exploit the trust of others had allowed him to claim the lives of countless young women, leaving a trail of devastation across the country. His pattern of deception and horror was unlike anything law enforcement had encountered before, forcing society to confront an unsettling truth: evil does not always look like a monster. Sometimes, it wears the face of a friend, a student, or even a charming stranger who just needs a little help.

The Trial: A Charmer in Court

Ted Bundy's trials were unlike anything the American justice system had seen before. A blend of courtroom drama, media spectacle, and psychological warfare, they were a stage for Bundy's manipulative charisma and arrogance. His legal battles not only exposed the gruesome details of his crimes but also revealed the unsettling power of his charm, even when faced with overwhelming evidence of his guilt. Bundy's trials showcased his ability to manipulate not only those in his immediate vicinity but also the public, who became captivated by the story of the "boy next door" turned killer.

Bundy's first trial stemmed from his 1975 arrest in Utah for the attempted abduction of Carol DaRonch. While he was convicted of this charge in 1976 and sentenced to prison, this was just the beginning of his legal entanglements. In 1977, Bundy was extradited to Colorado to face charges related to the murder of Caryn Campbell. It was during this time that Bundy's cunning and sense of superiority became glaringly evident. In June 1977, Bundy exploited a moment of inattention during a court proceeding and escaped from the Pitkin County Courthouse in Aspen. Having represented himself, Bundy had been allowed access to the courthouse law library, where he jumped from a second-story window and fled into the wilderness. His escape launched a massive manhunt and captivated the media, as law enforcement scrambled to apprehend the charming fugitive.

Bundy's escape was emblematic of his audacity and confidence in his ability to outsmart those around him. For six days, Bundy eluded capture, relying on his wits and physical endurance to survive in the mountains. However, his lack of preparation and supplies led to his recapture after he was spotted driving a stolen car. Despite this setback, Bundy's behaviour remained defiant. His courtroom antics during this period—including interrupting proceedings, challenging the judge, and mocking the prosecution—highlighted his belief in his intellectual superiority and his determination to control the narrative.

Bundy's second escape, in December 1977, was even more audacious and far-reaching in its consequences. This time, he managed to lose enough weight to squeeze through a hole in the ceiling of his cell at the Garfield County Jail. From there, he climbed into the crawlspace, broke into the apartment of a jailer, and walked out the front door wearing civilian clothes. It was a meticulously planned escape, and it worked. By the time his absence was discovered, Bundy was already on his way to Florida, where he would commit the most brutal and infamous murders of his criminal career.

Bundy's actions in Florida culminated in his arrest in February 1978, following the horrific attacks at the Chi Omega sorority house and the murder of 12-year-old Kimberly Leach. When Bundy was apprehended after a traffic stop in Pensacola, he initially refused to identify himself, further complicating the investigation. It wasn't until his fingerprints were matched that law enforcement realised they had one of the FBI's most wanted men in custody. His subsequent trial for the Chi Omega murders would mark the beginning of one of the most publicised courtroom dramas in American history.

The trial began in June 1979, and from the outset, Bundy's charm and arrogance were on full display. Having studied law during his time at the University of Utah, Bundy insisted on representing himself, rejecting the advice of his court-appointed attorneys. This decision allowed Bundy to control his narrative and turn the courtroom into a stage for his performance. He cross-examined witnesses, objected to the prosecution's arguments, and delivered his own opening and closing statements. Bundy's confidence in his abilities as a lawyer was astounding, particularly given the gravity of the charges against him. While some legal experts criticised his decision to act as his own counsel, others acknowledged the effectiveness of his tactics in sowing confusion and delaying the proceedings.

The Chi Omega trial was a media sensation, drawing national and international attention. Reporters flocked to the courtroom, eager to document every twist and turn of the case. Bundy's good looks and eloquence only heightened the public's fascination, particularly among women, many of whom viewed him as a misunderstood figure rather than a cold-blooded killer. The courtroom was frequently filled with female spectators who came not to seek justice but to catch a glimpse of the infamous Ted Bundy. Some even sent him love letters and marriage proposals, further illustrating the disturbing allure he held over certain members of the public.

Despite Bundy's theatrics, the evidence against him was overwhelming. Witnesses placed him near the scene of the crimes, and forensic evidence linked him directly to the murders. One of the most damning pieces of evidence was the bite mark analysis, which matched Bundy's teeth to marks found on one of the Chi Omega victims. Bundy, however, remained undeterred. He used his time in court to paint himself as a victim of a flawed justice system, claiming that he was being persecuted by a government determined to see him executed. His ability to spin his narrative and maintain his composure in the face of damning evidence was a testament to his manipulative prowess.

Throughout the trial, Bundy's behaviour oscillated between charm and defiance. He flirted with reporters, joked with the judge, and even proposed to his former girlfriend Carole Ann Boone during the penalty phase of the trial. Boone, who had testified on Bundy's behalf and believed in his innocence, accepted his proposal, further cementing Bundy's reputation as a master manipulator. The courtroom spectacle reached its peak when Bundy delivered an emotional closing argument, pleading with the jury to see him as a human being rather than a monster. Despite his efforts, the jury deliberated for less than seven hours before finding him guilty of the Chi Omega murders and sentencing him to death.

Bundy's conviction did little to diminish his confidence. In fact, he used his subsequent appeals as an opportunity to prolong his life and continue manipulating those around him. Bundy's legal manoeuvres stretched on for nearly a decade, as he filed motion after motion and acted as his own attorney in multiple hearings. During this time, he granted interviews to journalists and psychologists, using these interactions to craft his public image and maintain his notoriety. He frequently shifted between denying his guilt and offering partial confessions, depending on what he believed would benefit him most.

In 1986, Bundy faced another trial, this time for the murder of Kimberly Leach. Once again, Bundy's behaviour was erratic and self-serving. He used the trial as an opportunity to showcase his intelligence, but his arrogance ultimately alienated the jury. He was convicted and sentenced to death for the second time, further solidifying his fate. Despite this, Bundy continued to manipulate the legal system, filing appeals and requesting stays of execution. Each delay provided Bundy with more time to maintain his notoriety and play the role of the misunderstood genius.

The final chapter of Bundy's legal battles came in January 1989, when all of his appeals were exhausted, and his execution was scheduled. In the days leading up to his death, Bundy finally began to confess to some of his crimes, providing law enforcement with details about his victims and the locations of their bodies. These confessions were not acts of remorse but rather calculated attempts to delay his execution and assert control over his narrative. Even in his final moments, Bundy sought to manipulate those around him, offering just enough information to keep the authorities engaged without fully revealing the extent of his crimes.

Bundy was executed in the electric chair on January 24, 1989, at Florida State Prison. Outside the prison, crowds of spectators gathered to celebrate, holding signs that read "Burn, Bundy, Burn!" and "Justice for the Victims." The media frenzy surrounding his execution underscored the lasting impact of his crimes and the public's morbid fascination with his story. Even in death, Bundy remained a polarising figure, a man who had managed to charm and horrify in equal measure.

Ted Bundy's trials were not just legal proceedings—they were cultural phenomena that exposed the dark allure of a killer who defied stereotypes. His ability to manipulate the courtroom, the media, and the public demonstrated the power of charisma, even in the face of unimaginable evil. Bundy's performance in court was as much about maintaining his sense of control as it was about securing his freedom. For Bundy, the courtroom was not just a place of judgment; it was a stage where he could continue playing the role of the boy next door, even as the evidence revealed the monster beneath the mask.

Psychological Analysis: The Mind Behind the Mask

Ted Bundy's life and crimes continue to be studied not only because of their brutality but because of the chilling contradictions they reveal about human nature. How could someone so outwardly charismatic and intelligent commit such horrific acts? What allowed him to maintain such a convincing façade while engaging in behaviour that defied the very fabric of humanity? Exploring Bundy's psychology unveils the intricate mechanisms behind his deceit, manipulation, and violence, and forces us to confront uncomfortable truths about human behaviour and the potential for evil.

A Mask of Charm and Intelligence

Bundy's ability to navigate the world undetected for so long rested largely on his charisma and apparent normalcy. He was the embodiment of a societal archetype: the clean-cut, well-educated young man with a bright future. From an early age, Bundy learned to leverage this image to his advantage, using charm to deflect suspicion and manipulate those around him. This mask was not an accident—it was a carefully constructed tool, honed over years of observing human behaviour and exploiting vulnerabilities. Bundy's charm served as both a lure for his victims and a shield against accountability.

Psychologists have identified Bundy's charm as a hallmark of psychopathy, a personality disorder characterised by a lack of empathy, superficial charm, and an inflated sense of self-worth. Bundy's charm was superficial but convincing, allowing him to disarm even the most cautious individuals. He was a master of impression management, presenting himself as trustworthy and competent in social situations while hiding the darkness within. His ability to seamlessly transition between his "normal" persona and his predatory nature highlights the duality that defined his life.

Narcissism and the Need for Control

One of the most striking aspects of Bundy's personality was his narcissism. He exhibited an inflated sense of self-importance, believing himself to be superior to those around him. This belief underpinned much of his behaviour, from his courtroom antics to his manipulation of the media. Bundy saw himself as smarter and more cunning than his peers, law enforcement, and even his victims. His narcissism also drove his need for control, both over his environment and the people in it.

Control was a central theme in Bundy's crimes. His methods of luring and abducting victims were meticulously planned, designed to render his targets completely powerless. The physical acts of violence he inflicted—strangulation, bludgeoning, and post-mortem desecration—were all expressions of dominance and control. Even after his victims' deaths, Bundy would return to their bodies, reaffirming his power by engaging in necrophilic acts. This need to maintain control extended to his legal battles, where he insisted on representing himself, refusing to relinquish authority to anyone, even trained attorneys. Bundy's belief in his own superiority and his obsession with control were driving forces behind his actions.

The Absence of Empathy

Perhaps the most chilling aspect of Bundy's psyche was his complete lack of empathy. He viewed his victims not as human beings but as objects to be used for his gratification. This dehumanisation allowed him to commit unspeakable acts without remorse or hesitation. Bundy's inability to empathise with others is a key characteristic of psychopathy, a condition often associated with violent criminal behaviour. Psychopaths are unable to form genuine emotional connections, instead mimicking emotions to manipulate others.

Bundy's lack of empathy extended beyond his victims to everyone in his life. He used people as tools, exploiting their trust and affection to serve his own needs. His relationships with women, including Elizabeth Kloepfer and Carole Ann Boone, were marked by manipulation and deceit. While he presented himself as a loving partner, Bundy's actions revealed a man incapable of genuine love or concern. His relationships were transactional, providing him with validation and cover for his crimes.

Compartmentalisation and the Dual Life

Bundy's ability to lead a double life—charming friend and partner by day, remorseless killer by night—was rooted in his extraordinary capacity for compartmentalisation. This psychological mechanism allowed him to separate his violent impulses from his outward behaviour, maintaining the illusion of normalcy even as he committed horrific acts. Compartmentalisation is a coping strategy often used to reconcile conflicting aspects of one's identity, but in Bundy's case, it became a tool for concealing his true self.

Bundy's double life was meticulously maintained. He worked as a crisis hotline volunteer, offering comfort and support to people in their darkest moments, while simultaneously planning and executing his crimes. This stark contrast between his public and private personas baffled those who knew him. How could the man who saved lives at the hotline be the same person who took so many lives? The answer lies in Bundy's ability to suppress any cognitive dissonance, keeping his two worlds entirely separate.

Sadistic Pleasures and the Psychology of Violence

Bundy's crimes were not merely acts of violence—they were expressions of sadistic pleasure. He derived gratification from inflicting pain and terror, taking pleasure in the suffering of his victims. This sadism is another hallmark of psychopathy, reflecting a complete disregard for the well-being of others. Bundy's methods of killing were intimate and personal, involving physical overpowering and prolonged suffering. For Bundy, the act of killing was not just about ending a life; it was about asserting dominance and fulfilling his twisted fantasies.

The post-mortem acts Bundy committed, including necrophilia and mutilation, further illustrate the depth of his depravity. These behaviours were not necessary for the act of killing but were instead a means of extending his control over his victims even in death. By returning to the bodies and engaging in these acts, Bundy reaffirmed his power, reducing his victims to objects that existed solely for his gratification. This need for domination and control extended beyond his crimes to his interactions with law enforcement, the media, and even his trial.

The Role of Fantasy and Escalation

Bundy's crimes did not emerge in a vacuum; they were the culmination of years of violent fantasies that escalated over time. Research on serial killers has shown that fantasy plays a central role in the development of their behaviour. Bundy's early exposure to violent pornography, combined with his feelings of inadequacy and rejection, likely fuelled his fantasies of domination and control. As he grew older, these fantasies became more detailed and compelling, eventually driving him to act on them.

The escalation of Bundy's crimes reflects the progression of his fantasies. His early crimes, such as the assault on Karen Sparks, were less calculated and more impulsive. However, as Bundy gained confidence, his methods became more refined and his attacks more brutal. Each successful crime reinforced his sense of power, creating a cycle of fantasy, action, and gratification that drove him to commit increasingly violent acts. Bundy's ability to escalate his behaviour while avoiding detection is a testament to his cunning and adaptability.

Ego and the Need for Recognition

Bundy's narcissism extended to a desire for recognition, even for his crimes. While he initially denied his guilt,

Bundy's later confessions revealed a man who took pride in his actions. He often spoke of his crimes with a sense of detachment, as though he were describing the actions of someone else. This detachment allowed him to maintain his composure while providing graphic details about his victims.

Bundy's need for recognition was also evident in his interactions with the media and law enforcement. He granted interviews to journalists, offering tantalising hints about his crimes while maintaining an air of mystery. These interviews served as a platform for Bundy to assert his intelligence and control, further feeding his ego. Even in his final days, Bundy used his confessions as a means of prolonging his life and keeping himself in the spotlight. His desire to be remembered, even as a monster, reflects the depth of his narcissism.

The Legacy of Ted Bundy's Psychology

Bundy's psychological profile has been the subject of extensive study, providing valuable insights into the minds of serial killers. His case highlights the importance of understanding the warning signs of psychopathy, narcissism, and other personality disorders. Bundy's ability to manipulate and deceive those around him underscores the danger of relying solely on outward appearances to assess character.

While Bundy's crimes were uniquely horrific, the psychological mechanisms that drove him are not uncommon. His story serves as a reminder that evil does not always manifest in obvious ways. The mind behind the mask is often far more complex—and far more dangerous—than we might imagine. Bundy's legacy is one of terror, but it is also a cautionary tale about the potential for darkness that lies within human nature.

Legacy: Lessons from the Boy Next Door

Ted Bundy's crimes left a profound and lasting impact, not only on the families of his victims but on society as a whole. His legacy is one of terror, manipulation, and betrayal, but it is also one that offers valuable lessons about human behaviour, law enforcement, and the vulnerabilities of societal trust. Bundy's ability to hide in plain sight, blending seamlessly into communities and exploiting cultural norms, continues to serve as a chilling reminder that evil can wear an unassuming face. His story reshaped how we perceive danger, altered investigative practices, and challenged society to confront the uncomfortable truth that appearances can be deceiving.

Redefining the Face of Evil

Before Bundy, the archetype of a killer in the public imagination was someone visibly sinister or abnormal—an outcast whose malevolence was evident to those around them. Bundy shattered this stereotype. Handsome, intelligent, and articulate, he defied every preconceived notion of what a murderer should look like. This was not the deranged figure lurking in dark alleys; this was a man who volunteered at crisis hotlines, charmed his professors, and carried himself with the confidence of someone destined for success. Bundy's crimes forced society to confront the unsettling reality that evil does not always come with a warning sign.

Bundy's duality—the outward charm and inward monstrosity—changed how law enforcement, psychologists, and the public approached the concept of criminal behaviour. He demonstrated that dangerous individuals are not always immediately recognisable and that their capacity for manipulation can make them even more dangerous. This revelation was both terrifying and illuminating, reshaping public awareness about trusting first impressions and superficial qualities.

Lessons for Law Enforcement

Bundy's case highlighted significant flaws in law enforcement practices of the time, particularly in terms of communication and inter-agency cooperation. Bundy's ability to operate across multiple states, abducting and murdering women in Washington, Utah, Colorado, Idaho, and Florida, was made possible by the fragmented nature of criminal investigations. During the 1970s, there was no centralised system for tracking crimes across jurisdictions, allowing Bundy to evade detection even as his crimes followed a consistent pattern.

The Bundy case became a catalyst for change. One of the most significant developments was the creation of the Violent Criminal Apprehension Program (ViCAP) by the FBI in 1985. This database allows law enforcement agencies to share and cross-reference information about violent crimes, making it easier to identify patterns and link cases that occur in different jurisdictions. Bundy's case was also instrumental in the rise of behavioural profiling, as FBI profilers began studying his methods and motivations to develop a better understanding of serial offenders. The insights gained from Bundy's crimes have since been used to apprehend other serial killers, saving countless lives.

Media and the Cult of Personality

Bundy's trial was one of the first to be heavily covered by television, marking a turning point in the relationship between crime and the media. The spectacle of the "charming killer" captivated audiences, with Bundy's good looks, charisma, and theatrical courtroom behaviour drawing in viewers from around the world. This intense media focus turned Bundy into a macabre celebrity, a phenomenon that raised questions about the ethics of sensationalising criminal cases.

The media's portrayal of Bundy contributed to a dangerous fascination with his personality, overshadowing the horror of his crimes. Women flocked to his trials, some convinced of his innocence, others seemingly enamoured by his charm. This public response revealed a disturbing societal tendency to romanticise dangerous men, particularly those who fit conventional standards of attractiveness and intelligence. The Bundy phenomenon has since been replicated with other high-profile criminals, underscoring the need for responsible reporting and a focus on victims rather than perpetrators.

At the same time, the widespread coverage of Bundy's trial also served an educational purpose, raising awareness about the importance of vigilance and the reality of predatory behaviour. For many, Bundy became a cautionary figure, a reminder that trust should not be given lightly and that appearances can be dangerously deceptive.

Cultural Impact: The Enduring Fascination

The cultural impact of Ted Bundy cannot be overstated. Decades after his execution, his story continues to captivate the public, inspiring books, documentaries, films, and podcasts. This enduring fascination stems from the contradictions inherent in Bundy's character: the polished exterior masking a monstrous core. People are drawn to his story because it forces them to grapple with the complexities of human nature and the fragility of trust.

At the same time, this fascination has sparked important discussions about how we remember and portray serial killers. Critics argue that the focus on Bundy's charm and intelligence risks glorifying his crimes, overshadowing the suffering of his victims. In response, many contemporary accounts of Bundy's story have shifted their focus, centring the experiences of his victims and the families left behind. This shift reflects a broader societal effort to humanise the victims of violent crime and ensure that their stories are not lost amid the allure of a charismatic perpetrator.

Psychological Lessons: The Mask of Deception

One of the most significant lessons from Bundy's legacy lies in the understanding of psychopathy and manipulation. Bundy was a textbook example of a psychopath, exhibiting traits such as superficial charm, a lack of empathy, and a grandiose sense of self-worth. His ability to mimic normalcy and exploit societal expectations revealed the dangerous potential of these traits when combined with violent tendencies.

Psychologists and criminologists have studied Bundy extensively, using his case to better understand how psychopaths operate and how they can be identified. Bundy's manipulation of his victims, law enforcement, and even his own defence team showcased the lengths to which he was willing to go to maintain control. His case highlighted the importance of recognising red flags, such as a history of lying, a lack of genuine emotional connections, and a pattern of exploiting others for personal gain.

Bundy's crimes also underscored the need to challenge societal biases and assumptions. Many of Bundy's victims were lured by his appearance of vulnerability—a man with a sling or crutches asking for help. This ruse worked because it exploited deeply ingrained social norms about kindness and trust. His ability to exploit these norms serves as a reminder that predators often use societal expectations to their advantage, and that vigilance and critical thinking are essential in assessing potentially dangerous situations.

The Victims' Legacy

While Bundy's name dominates discussions of his crimes, it is essential to remember the victims who lost their lives to his violence. Each woman he murdered was an individual with hopes, dreams, and loved ones, and their stories deserve to be at the forefront of his legacy. Over the years, efforts have been made to honour Bundy's victims, from memorials to initiatives aimed at preventing violence against women.

The stories of Bundy's victims also highlight systemic issues that persist to this day, including the societal pressures that make women particularly vulnerable to predatory behaviour. Bundy preyed on the kindness and trust of his victims, targeting those who were willing to help a stranger in need. By examining the factors that allowed Bundy to operate undetected for so long, society can work to address the conditions that enable violence and protect potential victims.

The Uncomfortable Truths About Human Nature

Bundy's story forces us to confront uncomfortable truths about human nature and the potential for darkness within us all. His ability to lead a double life, appearing as a kind and capable individual while committing acts of unimaginable cruelty, raises questions about the nature of evil and the thin line that separates normalcy from monstrosity. Bundy's crimes challenge us to reflect on the ways in which society rewards superficial qualities—good looks, charm, intelligence—while ignoring deeper warning signs.

At its core, Bundy's legacy is a reminder of the complexity of human behaviour. He was not a caricature of evil but a deeply flawed individual who embodied the extremes of human potential. Understanding Bundy's psychology and the societal factors that allowed him to thrive can help us better navigate the complexities of trust, vulnerability, and the human condition.

A Legacy of Vigilance and Awareness

Ultimately, Ted Bundy's legacy serves as both a warning and a call to action. His crimes exposed the vulnerabilities of a society that places too much emphasis on appearances and stereotypes, and his ability to evade capture for so long highlighted the need for systemic improvements in law enforcement. While Bundy's story is one of horror, it has also inspired progress, from advances in criminal profiling to the creation of systems designed to track and apprehend serial offenders.

The lessons from Bundy's life and crimes are clear: appearances can be deceiving, trust must be earned, and vigilance is essential. By learning from the past, we can honour the victims who lost their lives and work to create a safer and more just society. Ted Bundy's story is a chilling reminder of the darkness that can hide behind the most ordinary of masks—and the enduring need to look beyond the surface.

2
The Clown With a Dark Secret – John Wayne Gacy

When delving into the chilling world of true crime, few names evoke the same level of dread and morbid curiosity as John Wayne Gacy. Known as the "Killer Clown," Gacy's crimes shocked the world not only because of their sheer brutality but also because of the unsettling duality of his life—a man who wore a painted smile by day and concealed unimaginable horrors by night. His story remains one of the darkest chapters in the annals of American crime, a tale that continues to haunt the public imagination.

Gacy was the epitome of the wolf in sheep's clothing. A well-liked community figure, he hosted neighbourhood parties, dressed as "Pogo the Clown" to entertain children, and even rubbed shoulders with politicians. Yet, beneath this facade lay a predator who lured young men and boys into his orbit, trapping them in a web of deceit, torture, and ultimately, death. The discovery of 29 bodies buried beneath his suburban Chicago home revealed the grim extent of his atrocities, making Gacy one of the most prolific serial killers in history.

In these chapters, we will peel back the layers of Gacy's life to uncover the events, relationships, and psychological patterns that led to his descent into monstrosity. From his seemingly ordinary childhood in the Midwest to the sinister rituals that became his modus operandi, each piece of the puzzle brings us closer to understanding the man behind the mask.

But this is not just a story of murder. It is a study of manipulation, charm, and the cracks in a society that allowed Gacy to operate unchecked for so long. We will also explore the investigation that finally brought him to justice, the tireless work of detectives who connected the dots, and the survivors who bravely shared their stories.

John Wayne Gacy's tale is a sobering reminder of the darkness that can lurk behind even the most ordinary of facades. As we journey into his life and crimes, prepare to confront the unsettling truth: monsters rarely look like monsters. Sometimes, they wear a smile.

Early Life and Troubled Foundations

John Wayne Gacy Jr. was born on March 17, 1942, in Chicago, Illinois, to John Stanley Gacy and Marion Elaine Robinson. As the middle child in a family of three, he grew up in a working-class Polish-American neighbourhood on the northwest side of Chicago. This post-war suburban environment, characterised by modest homes and strong family values, seemed to epitomise the American dream. However, within the Gacy household, the reality was far from ideal, and the seeds of a deeply troubled psyche were sown.

Central to Gacy's early struggles was his relationship with his father, John Stanley Gacy, a World War I veteran and machinist. Gacy Sr. was a strict disciplinarian who ruled the household with an iron fist, believing that toughness and authority were the marks of a man. Unfortunately, this belief manifested in physical abuse and constant belittlement, particularly aimed at his only son. From a young age, John Wayne Gacy was subjected to verbal assaults, frequently being called "sissy" or "mama's boy" by his father, who viewed him as weak and incapable of meeting his rigid standards of masculinity.

Compounding his father's scorn was Gacy's physical frailty. As a child, he suffered from a congenital heart condition that caused frequent blackouts and limited his ability to participate in physical activities. These health issues set him apart from other boys and made him the target of his father's ire. Gacy also experienced a head injury at the age of eleven when he was struck by a swing, an event that left him unconscious and could have had lasting effects on his brain. The combination of these physical challenges and his father's relentless criticism left Gacy feeling inadequate and unworthy of love.

The abuse in the Gacy household went beyond harsh words. Gacy Sr.'s punishments often turned violent, with physical beatings being a regular occurrence. He would use belts or his bare hands to discipline John for perceived infractions, sometimes administering these punishments in front of his siblings or friends, adding public humiliation to the physical pain. Despite this harsh treatment, Gacy desperately sought his father's approval. He longed for recognition and validation, but his efforts were continually dismissed or ridiculed. This relentless rejection left deep emotional scars and instilled in Gacy a need to seek approval from others, a trait that would define his adult relationships.

In contrast to his father's cruelty, Gacy's mother, Marion, provided him with unconditional love and support. She often acted as a buffer between her husband's temper and her son's vulnerabilities, stepping in to protect John from the worst of his father's wrath. Marion's affection offered Gacy a sense of safety and comfort, but it also deepened the divide between him and his father. Gacy Sr. resented what he perceived as Marion's coddling of their son, blaming her for John's perceived shortcomings. This dynamic created a toxic family environment where Gacy was caught between his mother's nurturing and his father's condemnation.

During his adolescence, Gacy faced additional struggles that further compounded his sense of isolation. He began to experience feelings of sexual confusion, which he kept hidden out of fear of judgment and rejection. Growing up in a conservative, mid-20th-century environment, any deviation from traditional gender norms was met with suspicion and scorn. For Gacy, who was already grappling with his father's accusations of being effeminate, these feelings only added to his shame. Around this time, Gacy was also sexually abused by a family acquaintance, a contractor who assaulted him on multiple occasions. This abuse, which Gacy never disclosed to his family, further deepened his feelings of powerlessness and betrayal.

Despite the challenges at home and his internal struggles, Gacy worked hard to maintain a facade of normalcy. In school, he was described as friendly and likable, though academically unremarkable. His grades suffered, possibly due to undiagnosed learning disabilities or the lingering effects of his childhood injuries. However, Gacy excelled in social situations, displaying an eagerness to please and an ability to charm those around him. This adaptability became a defining feature of his personality, allowing him to mask his insecurities and gain the trust of others.

As Gacy grew older, his desperation to escape his father's control intensified. He took on part-time jobs and became involved in community activities, seeking validation and recognition outside the home. Yet no matter what he achieved, his father's approval remained out of reach. Even small accomplishments were dismissed as insignificant or mocked outright. This relentless invalidation reinforced Gacy's belief that he was fundamentally flawed, a belief that would shape his adult life in profound and disturbing ways.

The Double Life Begins

By the time John Wayne Gacy entered adulthood, the foundations of his personality had been set. He was deeply insecure, shaped by years of emotional and physical abuse from his father, yet adept at presenting a polished, agreeable persona to the world. His desire for approval, paired with his internal struggles, created a man capable of living two lives: one that appeared charming, kind, and socially engaged, and another marked by secrecy, manipulation, and dark desires. This duplicity began to crystallise as Gacy transitioned into adulthood, laying the groundwork for the more sinister aspects of his later life.

In the early 1960s, Gacy moved to Springfield, Illinois, where he enrolled in a business college. He excelled in this environment, earning a diploma in business and immediately finding work in management. His natural charisma, ability to network, and eagerness to please made him successful in professional settings. Soon after, he relocated to Las Vegas, Nevada, and briefly worked as an attendant at a funeral home. This job marked one of the first instances of his disturbing tendencies emerging. Gacy later confessed to having climbed into a coffin with a deceased teenage boy, where he experienced an unsettling sense of arousal. Though he claimed he did not act on this impulse, the event hinted at the darker urges that lurked beneath his outwardly normal demeanour.

By 1964, Gacy returned to Illinois and settled in Chicago, where he became a manager at a shoe company. It was during this period that he met Marlynn Myers, a co-worker who would later become his first wife. Marlynn came from a well-connected family that owned multiple Kentucky Fried Chicken (KFC) franchises in Waterloo, Iowa. The couple married in September 1964, and Marlynn's parents offered Gacy an opportunity to manage three of their KFC restaurants in Waterloo. This move marked a turning point in Gacy's life, as it allowed him to assume a new role as a respected business leader and family man. Eager to escape the shadow of his father and build a successful life, Gacy embraced the opportunity and relocated to Iowa with his new wife.

Waterloo offered Gacy the chance to reinvent himself. He quickly became a prominent figure in the local community, joining civic organisations and volunteering his time to charitable causes. Among these was the local chapter of the Jaycees, a national organisation dedicated to developing leadership skills in young men. Gacy's charm and ambition made him a standout member, and he soon rose to leadership positions within the group. To those who knew him during this time, Gacy appeared to be the embodiment of the American dream: a successful businessman, devoted husband, and engaged community member. Yet beneath this facade, the cracks were beginning to show.

While Gacy's involvement with the Jaycees bolstered his public image, it also provided him with access to a world of indulgence and secrecy. The Waterloo chapter of the Jaycees was known for its hedonistic culture, which included heavy drinking, drug use, and even organised wife-swapping parties. Gacy not only participated in these activities but actively embraced them, further cultivating his ability to live a double life. Publicly, he remained a committed family man and community leader, but privately, he began exploring his darker desires.

It was during this time that Gacy's predatory tendencies began to emerge. He used his position within the Jaycees and his role as a business manager to gain the trust of young men and teenage boys, often employing them at his KFC franchises. Gacy's charisma and charm made him approachable, and many of his employees saw him as a mentor figure. However, he used this trust to exploit them, luring boys into compromising situations under the guise of offering advice or support. In one instance, Gacy invited a teenage boy to his home, plied him with alcohol, and then sexually assaulted him. Despite his outward appearance as a respectable community member, Gacy was beginning to reveal his predatory nature in private.

In 1968, Gacy's double life came crashing down when he was arrested and charged with sexually assaulting a teenage boy. The victim, who had been lured to Gacy's home under the pretext of discussing job opportunities, reported the incident to the police. As the investigation unfolded, additional victims came forward with similar allegations. Gacy vehemently denied the charges, claiming the accusations were part of a conspiracy orchestrated by his political rivals within the Jaycees. However, the evidence against him was overwhelming, and he ultimately pleaded guilty to sodomy.

Gacy was sentenced to ten years in prison at the Anamosa State Penitentiary in Iowa. His incarceration marked a significant blow to the life he had carefully constructed. Marlynn divorced him shortly after his sentencing, taking their two children and severing ties with Gacy completely. Publicly disgraced and abandoned by his family, Gacy was forced to confront the consequences of his actions. Yet, even in prison, he continued to cultivate his ability to manipulate and charm those around him.

During his time at Anamosa, Gacy was a model prisoner. He earned the trust of the prison staff, took on leadership roles, and even organised events for his fellow inmates. His good behaviour earned him parole after just 18 months, a fraction of his original sentence. Gacy's early release was a testament to his ability to present himself as a rehabilitated and trustworthy individual, despite the crimes that had landed him in prison. However, his time behind bars did little to curb his predatory impulses. Instead, it gave him the opportunity to refine his tactics and better conceal his darker tendencies.

Upon his release from prison in 1970, Gacy returned to Chicago to live with his mother. He was determined to rebuild his life and quickly set about establishing a new identity. Within months, he secured a job as a construction contractor and began to re-establish himself as a respectable member of society. Gacy's natural charisma and work ethic made him successful in his new career, and he soon started his own construction business, PDM Contractors. The company became a key part of Gacy's public persona, allowing him to present himself as a hardworking entrepreneur while providing a cover for his increasingly sinister activities.

In 1972, Gacy remarried, tying the knot with Carole Hoff, a divorcee with two daughters. The marriage further solidified his image as a family man, and the couple settled into a modest home in Norwood Park, a quiet suburban neighbourhood on the outskirts of Chicago. To his neighbours, Gacy was friendly and generous, often hosting elaborate parties and dressing up as "Pogo the Clown" to entertain children at local events. This clown persona would later become one of the most infamous aspects of his double life, symbolising the horrifying dichotomy between his public image and his private actions.

Gacy's construction business not only provided financial stability but also gave him access to a steady stream of young male employees, many of whom were vulnerable and easy to exploit. He often hired teenagers and young men who were down on their luck, offering them mentorship and a sense of belonging. However, these acts of generosity were often a prelude to manipulation and abuse. Gacy would lure his employees into his home under the guise of discussing work or providing mentorship, only to drug or overpower them.

Despite his increasingly brazen behaviour, Gacy's public persona remained untarnished. He became involved in local politics, joining the Democratic Party and even posing for photographs with prominent politicians. His ability to navigate these social circles further insulated him from suspicion, as few could imagine that the jovial, community-minded contractor was capable of such heinous acts. This period marked the height of Gacy's double life, as he successfully balanced his public image with his private atrocities.

Pogo the Clown and the Perfect Façade

John Wayne Gacy's life in the mid-1970s was a study in contrasts. By all outward appearances, he was a successful businessman, a dedicated community leader, and a devoted family man. He was known for his generosity, charisma, and willingness to help his neighbours and friends. Among the many facets of his public persona, his role as "Pogo the Clown" stood out as both endearing and memorable. Dressing up as a jovial clown to entertain children at local events, Gacy cultivated an image of warmth and altruism that masked the darkness lurking beneath. Pogo the Clown, however, was more than just a costume or hobby—it became a symbol of the two lives Gacy led, embodying the stark dichotomy between his public image and his secret depravity.

In the early 1970s, Gacy's life seemed to be stabilising after his release from prison and his move back to Chicago. He had remarried and started his own construction business, PDM Contractors, which became a success. As a way to further ingratiate himself with his community, Gacy became involved in local events, volunteering his time and resources to neighbourhood projects and Democratic Party campaigns. He joined civic organisations and was known for hosting elaborate parties at his home. These efforts cemented his reputation as a pillar of the community, a man who gave freely of his time and energy to those around him.

It was during this period that Gacy created his clown persona, Pogo. He joined the "Jolly Joker Clown Club," a group of amateur clowns who performed at hospitals, schools, and charity events. Gacy embraced the role with enthusiasm, designing his own elaborate clown costumes and makeup. His signature look featured a brightly coloured jumpsuit, oversized red shoes, and a painted face that included exaggerated red lips and sharp, angular eyes. Pogo's distinctive appearance was both playful and unsettling, a reflection of Gacy's own dual nature.

Gacy often performed as Pogo at children's birthday parties, local parades, and charity fundraisers. He relished the attention and praise he received in this role, enjoying the opportunity to bring joy to others while simultaneously enhancing his public image. To those who knew him as Pogo, Gacy appeared to be a kind-hearted man who delighted in entertaining children and giving back to his community. Yet, even in his clown persona, there were subtle hints of the darkness within. Gacy later admitted that dressing as Pogo gave him a sense of power and freedom, as if the costume allowed him to shed societal expectations and explore his darker impulses without fear of judgment.

By the mid-1970s, Gacy had fully embraced the duality of his life, carefully constructing and maintaining the perfect facade. His public image as a successful entrepreneur and community leader provided him with the social capital and trust he needed to conceal his private activities. Gacy was well-liked by his neighbours in Norwood Park, a quiet suburban neighbourhood on the outskirts of Chicago. He was known for being generous with his time and resources, often lending tools or offering help with home improvement projects. His parties were a highlight of the neighbourhood, drawing large crowds of friends, colleagues, and even local politicians.

Gacy's involvement in local politics further solidified his reputation as a respected member of the community. A staunch Democrat, he became active in precinct-level organising and worked on campaigns for prominent politicians. In one particularly notable instance, Gacy was photographed with First Lady Rosalynn Carter during a local event, wearing a pin that identified him as part of the event's organising committee. This photograph would later become infamous, symbolising how deeply embedded Gacy was in the fabric of his community.

Behind the scenes, however, Gacy was living a very different life. He used his construction business, PDM Contractors, as a means to lure vulnerable young men into his orbit. Many of his employees were teenagers or young adults who were down on their luck or looking for a fresh start. Gacy would hire these individuals under the guise of offering them legitimate work and mentorship, only to exploit their trust for his own purposes. His charm and seemingly friendly demeanour made it easy for him to gain the trust of his employees, many of whom saw him as a father figure or role model.

Pogo the Clown became more than just a persona for John Wayne Gacy; it was a symbol of his ability to manipulate appearances and obscure his true nature. While Gacy presented himself as a loving entertainer who brought joy to children, the reality was far darker. He later admitted that dressing as Pogo gave him a sense of liberation and anonymity, allowing him to express parts of himself that he felt were otherwise suppressed. In some ways, Pogo represented Gacy's understanding of himself: outwardly cheerful and entertaining, but inwardly chaotic and sinister.

The clown persona also served a practical purpose in Gacy's double life. It allowed him to embed himself in social situations where he could observe and interact with potential victims without raising suspicion. Pogo's disarming presence made Gacy seem approachable and harmless, which only enhanced his ability to gain the trust of young men and boys. The sharp contrast between the playful clown and the predator beneath underscores the chilling complexity of Gacy's character.

One of the most remarkable aspects of Gacy's double life was his ability to maintain the illusion of normalcy even as his crimes escalated. By the late 1970s, Gacy had begun a series of murders that would make him one of the most prolific serial killers in American history. Despite the mounting number of victims, he continued to lead a highly public life, attending political events, hosting parties, and performing as Pogo the Clown. His ability to compartmentalise his actions and maintain his facade speaks to his extraordinary capacity for manipulation and deceit.

Gacy's public persona also provided him with a level of protection that allowed him to evade suspicion for years. His neighbours and colleagues, charmed by his friendly demeanour and community involvement, could not reconcile the idea of Gacy the predator with the man they knew. This cognitive dissonance made it easier for Gacy to continue his crimes undetected, as those around him were unwilling or unable to see the signs of his true nature.

As Gacy's crimes grew more brazen, the cracks in his facade began to show. By the late 1970s, several people in his orbit had begun to notice odd or troubling behaviours. Some of his employees reported feeling uncomfortable around Gacy or sensing that something was "off" about him. Others noted the strange smells emanating from his home, which Gacy attributed to plumbing issues. Despite these warning signs, Gacy's public persona remained intact, and he continued to use his charm and social connections to deflect suspicion.

The eventual unravelling of Gacy's double life began with the disappearance of Robert Piest, a teenage boy who vanished in December 1978 after meeting with Gacy about a potential job. Piest's disappearance set off a chain of events that led to Gacy's arrest and the horrifying discovery of 29 bodies buried beneath his home. The revelation of Gacy's crimes shocked the nation and left those who had known him struggling to reconcile the man they thought they knew with the monster he truly was.

The Killing Spree

The true horror of John Wayne Gacy's life unfolded between 1972 and 1978, a six-year period during which he carried out a killing spree that left at least 33 young men and boys dead. During this time, Gacy perfected a gruesome method of luring, capturing, and murdering his victims, all while maintaining his outward appearance as a respected community member and successful businessman. The scale of his crimes, the systematic way in which he carried them out, and the chilling duplicity of his public and private lives have made Gacy one of the most infamous serial killers in history. The killing spree not only revealed Gacy's capacity for violence but also exposed the societal blind spots that allowed him to evade detection for so long.

Gacy's modus operandi evolved over time, but it always involved a calculated exploitation of trust and vulnerability. Many of his victims were teenagers or young men who were struggling financially, estranged from their families, or simply looking for work. Gacy would often meet these individuals through his construction business, PDM Contractors, where he employed a steady stream of young men to perform odd jobs. To those he targeted, Gacy appeared to be a kind and approachable figure—someone offering opportunities and mentorship. However, his true intentions were far more sinister.

Once Gacy gained his victims' trust, he would lure them to his home in Norwood Park under various pretences, such as offering them alcohol, drugs, or a chance to discuss work. Inside his home, he employed a series of tactics to disarm and control his victims. One of his most infamous methods involved performing a "magic trick" with handcuffs. Gacy, dressed as his clown persona or simply as himself, would convince his victims to let him demonstrate how to escape from the cuffs. Once the handcuffs were securely fastened on the victim, Gacy would reveal that there was no trick at all. "The trick," he chillingly told his victims, "is you have to have the key."

After restraining his victims, Gacy would torture them, often over the course of several hours. His methods included physical assault, strangulation, and, in some cases, sexual assault. He frequently used a rope garrotte, tightening it around his victim's neck until they suffocated. This deliberate and calculated method of killing demonstrated Gacy's complete lack of empathy and his enjoyment of exerting control over his victims.

As Gacy's killing spree continued, he needed a place to dispose of his victims' bodies. He initially buried them in the crawlspace beneath his home, a dark, cramped area that would eventually become one of the most infamous crime scenes in history. Over time, the crawlspace became so overcrowded with bodies that Gacy began running out of room. In some cases, he dismembered the bodies to fit them into smaller spaces or simply placed them in nearby areas of his property. The foul smell of decomposition permeated his home, a fact that Gacy dismissed to visitors as a plumbing issue.

The use of the crawlspace reflects not only Gacy's disregard for his victims but also his audacious belief that he could continue killing without consequence. The proximity of the bodies to his living space underscores the chilling compartmentalisation of his psyche—he was able to live, work, and socialise above the remains of his victims as if nothing was amiss.

Gacy's killing spree escalated as his confidence grew. By the mid-1970s, he had refined his methods and developed a disturbing level of efficiency in carrying out his crimes. The frequency of the murders increased, with multiple victims disappearing in quick succession. This escalation was driven in part by Gacy's growing sense of invincibility. He had managed to evade detection for years, despite mounting evidence that something was amiss.

One key factor that enabled Gacy's spree was the societal attitude toward missing persons during the 1970s. Many of Gacy's victims were young men from disadvantaged backgrounds or who had run away from home. Police often dismissed their disappearances as voluntary, assuming they had left their families to seek independence or adventure. This indifference allowed Gacy to continue preying on vulnerable individuals without attracting significant attention.

In addition, Gacy's public persona provided him with a shield of credibility. His involvement in local politics and community events gave him an air of respectability that made it difficult for others to believe he could be capable of such atrocities. Even when accusations were made or suspicions raised, Gacy was often able to talk his way out of trouble, using his charm and social connections to deflect scrutiny.

The victims of Gacy's killing spree were primarily teenage boys and young men, many of whom were lured into his orbit by promises of work, mentorship, or companionship. They ranged in age from 14 to their early 20s and came from diverse backgrounds, but most shared a common vulnerability: they were either estranged from their families, struggling financially, or seeking a sense of belonging.

Each victim had a story, a life cut tragically short by Gacy's actions. Among the more well-known victims was Timothy McCoy, believed to be Gacy's first murder victim. McCoy, a 16-year-old hitchhiker, was killed in 1972 after Gacy claimed he acted in self-defence during a struggle. In reality, McCoy had been lured to Gacy's home, where he was brutally attacked and murdered. This killing marked the beginning of Gacy's descent into serial murder, setting a pattern that he would repeat with chilling consistency.

Other victims included John Butkovich, a 17-year-old employee of Gacy's who disappeared after confronting him over unpaid wages, and Robert Piest, a 15-year-old who vanished after meeting Gacy about a job opportunity. Piest's disappearance would ultimately lead to Gacy's capture, but not before countless other lives were lost.

As Gacy's killing spree continued, his home in Norwood Park became a literal house of horrors. Visitors often remarked on the strange smells emanating from the property, which Gacy attributed to plumbing issues or moisture in the crawlspace. However, the truth was far more macabre. The crawlspace, which contained the remains of dozens of victims, was the epicentre of Gacy's crimes.

The process of disposing of the bodies was methodical and calculated. Gacy often enlisted the help of his employees to dig trenches in the crawlspace, claiming they were for drainage or structural work. In reality, these trenches were being prepared to conceal the bodies of his victims. Gacy's ability to involve others in this process, even unknowingly, highlights his manipulative nature and his capacity for compartmentalisation.

Gacy's killing spree began to unravel in December 1978 with the disappearance of Robert Piest. Piest, a high school student, went missing after meeting Gacy at a pharmacy where he worked. The teenager had told his mother that he was going to speak with a man about a job opportunity and would return shortly. When he failed to come home, his family immediately reported his disappearance to the police.

Unlike many of Gacy's previous victims, Piest came from a stable, supportive family that pushed authorities to investigate his disappearance thoroughly. The police quickly learned that Gacy was the last person to see Piest alive and began to dig deeper into his background. What they uncovered shocked even the most seasoned investigators.

As law enforcement gathered evidence and interviewed witnesses, Gacy's carefully constructed facade began to crumble. Surveillance of his home revealed erratic behaviour, and a search of his property eventually led to the discovery of human remains in the crawlspace. The scale of the horror became clear: Gacy had killed at least 33 young men and boys, most of whom were buried beneath his home.

The Investigation and Capture

The capture of John Wayne Gacy, one of the most prolific and notorious serial killers in American history, was the result of determined police work, mounting evidence, and a sequence of critical mistakes by Gacy himself. His arrest in December 1978 marked the culmination of years of unchecked violence and deceit. This chapter explores how Gacy's carefully constructed facade began to crack, the methods employed by law enforcement to uncover his crimes, and the chilling revelations that followed his arrest.

The chain of events that ultimately led to Gacy's capture began with the disappearance of 15-year-old Robert Piest. On the evening of December 11, 1978, Piest, a high school student in Des Plaines, Illinois, was working at a local pharmacy. He told his mother he was going to meet a man about a potential job opportunity and would return shortly. The man in question was John Wayne Gacy, a local contractor who had visited the pharmacy earlier that day to discuss a remodelling project with the owner. Gacy had mentioned to the pharmacy staff that he paid teenage boys $5 an hour—much higher than minimum wage—for work at his construction company, PDM Contractors.

When Robert failed to return home that evening, his family immediately grew concerned. Unlike many of Gacy's previous victims, who were often estranged from their families or had transient lifestyles, Robert came from a stable and loving home. His parents reported his disappearance to the Des Plaines Police Department the same night, triggering an investigation that would uncover the depths of Gacy's crimes.

Des Plaines police quickly learned that Gacy was the last person known to have seen Robert alive. They contacted him on December 12, 1978, to ask about the boy's disappearance. Gacy denied meeting Piest and claimed he had no information about his whereabouts.

However, officers were immediately suspicious. Gacy's demeanour was defensive and evasive, and when they ran a background check on him, they discovered his 1968 conviction for sodomy in Iowa. This revelation raised red flags, prompting the police to take a closer look at Gacy.

On December 13, detectives obtained a search warrant for Gacy's home in Norwood Park. The search revealed several suspicious items, including a receipt from the pharmacy where Robert Piest worked and a box of pornography that featured young boys. While the initial search did not uncover any direct evidence linking Gacy to Piest's disappearance, it strengthened the police's belief that he was involved. They began round-the-clock surveillance of Gacy, determined to keep him under close watch while they gathered more evidence.

For the next several days, a team of detectives followed Gacy's every move. The surveillance team, made up of two rotating shifts, monitored Gacy as he went about his daily life. He continued to attend meetings, visit restaurants, and socialise with friends, seemingly unfazed by the police presence. However, as the surveillance continued, Gacy's behaviour grew increasingly erratic. He began driving aimlessly around the Chicago area, often for hours at a time, as if trying to lose the officers tailing him. On several occasions, he invited members of the surveillance team to join him for meals, displaying a disturbing mix of arrogance and audacity.

The psychological pressure of being watched 24/7 began to take its toll on Gacy. He became more agitated and reckless, making cryptic comments to acquaintances and even bragging to the police that they would never find anything to implicate him. However, his overconfidence ultimately worked against him, as he let his guard down and made critical mistakes that further incriminated him.

As the investigation progressed, the police began to piece together a clearer picture of Gacy's activities. They interviewed former employees of PDM Contractors, some of whom described unsettling encounters with Gacy. Several young men reported that Gacy had made unwanted advances or behaved inappropriately toward them. Others mentioned the frequent presence of teenage boys at his home, many of whom seemed to disappear without explanation.

Meanwhile, forensic evidence began to surface. A key breakthrough came when police linked a ring found in Gacy's home during the initial search to one of his previous victims, John Butkovich, a 17-year-old who had gone missing in 1976 after confronting Gacy about unpaid wages. This connection provided investigators with tangible proof that Gacy was involved in the disappearances of multiple young men.

Detectives also learned about the strange smells emanating from Gacy's home. Several neighbours and former employees mentioned the foul odour, which Gacy had dismissed as a plumbing issue. This detail raised suspicions that Gacy's home might hold the answers to the growing list of missing persons cases.

By December 21, 1978, the mounting evidence against Gacy allowed the police to obtain a second search warrant for his home. This time, investigators were prepared to dig deeper—literally. During the search, officers noticed a section of the floor in the crawlspace that appeared to have been recently disturbed. Using shovels, they began digging in the area and soon uncovered human remains. The discovery confirmed their worst fears: Gacy had been using his home as a burial site for his victims.

As the excavation continued, more bodies were unearthed, each one bearing signs of strangulation or other forms of violent death. The crawlspace contained a chilling network of trenches that Gacy had used to dispose of his victims. The discovery of these bodies sent shockwaves through the community and marked the beginning of the end for John Wayne Gacy.

Confronted with the overwhelming evidence, Gacy was arrested on December 21, 1978. During his initial interrogation, he continued to deny any involvement in the murders. However, as the questioning continued, Gacy began to unravel. The psychological pressure, combined with his growing realisation that his crimes were finally coming to light, led him to confess.

Over the course of several hours, Gacy provided detectives with a chilling account of his crimes. He admitted to murdering at least 33 young men and boys, most of whom he buried in the crawlspace of his home. He described his methods in horrifying detail, explaining how he lured his victims, restrained them with handcuffs, and used a rope garrotte to strangle them. Gacy showed no remorse during his confession, instead speaking about his crimes with a detached, almost clinical demeanour.

Gacy also admitted that he had run out of space in the crawlspace and had begun disposing of bodies in the Des Plaines River. This revelation led investigators to search the river and surrounding areas for additional remains, further expanding the scope of the investigation.

The discovery of the bodies and Gacy's confession sent shockwaves through the nation. The sheer scale of his crimes, combined with the grotesque details of how he carried them out, made him one of the most infamous serial killers in history. As the investigation continued, police worked tirelessly to identify the remains of Gacy's victims, many of whom had been reported missing years earlier. The process of identification was painstaking and relied on dental records, personal items, and, in some cases, DNA evidence.

Gacy's arrest also prompted widespread outrage and reflection on the societal factors that had allowed him to evade detection for so long. Many of his victims had been dismissed by police as runaways, and the lack of communication between law enforcement agencies in different jurisdictions had allowed Gacy to operate unchecked. His case highlighted the need for reforms in the way missing persons cases were handled and led to increased awareness of the vulnerabilities faced by young men and boys.

The Trial and Media Frenzy

The arrest of John Wayne Gacy in December 1978 and the subsequent discovery of 29 bodies buried in his crawlspace—and four others disposed of in nearby rivers—shocked the nation. As investigators uncovered the horrific details of his crimes, the media latched onto the case, sparking a public fascination with Gacy and his double life. By the time his trial began in February 1980, the sheer scale of his crimes and his disturbing clown persona as "Pogo" had cemented Gacy as one of America's most infamous serial killers. His trial was not just a legal proceeding; it became a media spectacle that captured the attention of the entire country.

After his arrest, John Wayne Gacy was charged with 33 counts of murder, making him one of the most prolific serial killers in American history. The sheer number of victims and the gruesome details of his crimes set Gacy apart from any other criminal case of the era. The public was captivated not only by the brutality of his actions but also by his ability to live a double life as a respected businessman and community member. The discovery of his crimes raised questions about how someone so seemingly normal could commit such heinous acts, adding to the intense public interest.

The pretrial period was marked by extensive media coverage, as journalists scrambled to uncover every detail about Gacy's life. His role as Pogo the Clown became a focal point of the narrative, with headlines emphasising the chilling juxtaposition of his cheerful public persona and his dark private life. The image of Gacy as a killer clown dominated the media, turning him into a symbol of hidden evil.

Gacy initially pleaded not guilty to the charges, and his defence team began preparing a strategy based on claims of insanity. His lawyers argued that Gacy's mental state at the time of the murders rendered him incapable of understanding the nature of his actions, a defence that would later become the central focus of the trial. Meanwhile, the prosecution worked to build a case that would show Gacy's actions were premeditated and methodical, undermining any claims of diminished responsibility.

On February 6, 1980, John Wayne Gacy's trial began at the Cook County Criminal Court in Chicago, Illinois. The courtroom was packed with reporters, journalists, and members of the public, all eager to witness the proceedings firsthand. Outside the courthouse, crowds of onlookers gathered, hoping to catch a glimpse of the man who had become the face of evil in America. The trial quickly became one of the most publicised in U.S. history, with newspapers and television networks providing daily updates on the case.

The prosecution, led by William Kunkle, presented a detailed and harrowing case against Gacy. They outlined how he had lured his victims to his home, restrained them using handcuffs, and tortured them before ultimately killing them. The prosecution presented forensic evidence, including photographs of the crawlspace where the bodies were buried, as well as items recovered from Gacy's home that linked him to his victims. Witness testimony played a crucial role in the trial, with several individuals recounting their interactions with Gacy and describing his manipulative and predatory behaviour.

One of the most damning pieces of evidence was Gacy's own confession, which he had given to police after his arrest. In it, he admitted to killing more than 30 young men and boys, describing his methods in chilling detail. The prosecution argued that Gacy's ability to recount his crimes so clearly demonstrated that he was fully aware of his actions and their consequences, directly countering the insanity defence.

The cornerstone of Gacy's defence was the claim that he was legally insane at the time of the murders. His defence team argued that he suffered from multiple personality disorder, with his homicidal actions being carried out by an alternate personality that he referred to as "Jack." They presented Gacy as a deeply disturbed individual who was unable to control his violent impulses due to his mental illness. To support this claim, the defence called psychiatrists and psychologists to testify about Gacy's mental state.

The defence attempted to paint a picture of Gacy's childhood and early life as factors that contributed to his mental instability. They highlighted the abuse he suffered at the hands of his father, as well as the sexual abuse he experienced as a teenager. These experiences, they argued, created a fractured psyche that ultimately led to his violent behaviour.

However, the prosecution countered these arguments by presenting evidence that Gacy was fully aware of his actions and had taken deliberate steps to conceal his crimes. They pointed out that Gacy had carefully planned the murders, going so far as to dig trenches in his crawlspace to bury the bodies. His ability to maintain a double life as a respected businessman and community leader also suggested a level of self-control that was inconsistent with the defence's claims of insanity.

As the trial progressed, media coverage of the case reached a fever pitch. Journalists reported on every development, from witness testimony to courtroom drama, and the public consumed the updates with morbid fascination. The trial became a cultural phenomenon, with Gacy's name and crimes dominating headlines across the country.

The image of Gacy as "The Killer Clown" was a particularly powerful narrative, capturing the public's imagination and solidifying his status as a symbol of hidden evil. His role as Pogo the Clown became a focal point of media coverage, with many articles and news segments using the clown persona as a way to highlight the contrast between Gacy's public image and his private actions.

The media frenzy surrounding the trial also led to intense scrutiny of the legal proceedings. Critics questioned whether the overwhelming publicity would make it impossible for Gacy to receive a fair trial. However, the presiding judge took steps to ensure the integrity of the process, including carefully selecting jurors who could remain impartial despite the extensive media coverage.

After weeks of testimony and deliberation, the jury reached a verdict on March 12, 1980. John Wayne Gacy was found guilty of 33 counts of murder, as well as additional charges related to sexual assault and the concealment of bodies. The verdict was unanimous, with the jury rejecting the insanity defence and concluding that Gacy had acted with full awareness of his actions.

The sentencing phase of the trial was equally swift. On March 13, Gacy was sentenced to death for his crimes, with the judge describing him as having committed "unimaginable horror" and calling him a "man without a soul." The sentence reflected the gravity of Gacy's crimes and the impact they had on his victims' families and the broader community.

The conclusion of Gacy's trial brought a sense of closure to many, but it also left lingering questions about how such atrocities could have occurred. The trial and media coverage highlighted systemic failures in law enforcement and society that allowed Gacy to operate unchecked for so long. Many of his victims had been dismissed as runaways, and the lack of communication between different police jurisdictions meant that patterns in the disappearances were not identified earlier.

The public's fascination with Gacy continued long after his trial, as he became the subject of books, documentaries, and films. His crimes sparked broader conversations about serial killers, mental health, and the vulnerabilities of marginalized individuals in society. Gacy's case also underscored the role of the media in shaping public perceptions of crime, with the "Killer Clown" narrative becoming an enduring symbol of hidden danger.

Prison Years and Legacy

After his conviction on March 13, 1980, John Wayne Gacy was sentenced to death for the murder of 33 young men and boys. The sentence was a reflection of the brutality of his crimes and the profound impact they had on the victims' families and society. Gacy's time on death row, however, would last for more than 14 years, during which he continued to manipulate public perception, protest his innocence, and cultivate a disturbing legacy. His imprisonment became a platform for self-promotion, manipulation, and deflection, and even in captivity, he managed to leave an indelible mark on American culture and the criminal justice system.

Following his sentencing, Gacy was sent to Illinois' Menard Correctional Centre, where he spent the majority of his time on death row. His incarceration, like much of his life, was marked by contradictions. On one hand, Gacy claimed to have reformed, presenting himself as a model prisoner who participated in various activities and maintained good behaviour. On the other hand, his time in prison was also characterised by his relentless denial of guilt and his disturbing attempts to control his narrative.

While awaiting execution, Gacy managed to build a relatively comfortable life within the confines of prison. He developed routines that included reading, writing letters, and painting, which would later become a significant part of his legacy. Despite being cut off from the outside world, Gacy maintained connections with supporters, media representatives, and even a morbidly fascinated public. He used these connections to continue spreading misinformation about his crimes, claiming that he was innocent and that the true number of victims had been exaggerated.

One of Gacy's primary activities in prison was his work as an artist. He took up painting as a hobby, creating a wide range of works that included self-portraits, landscapes, and, most infamously, depictions of clowns. Many of these paintings featured his alter ego, "Pogo the Clown," a persona that had already become synonymous with his crimes. Gacy's artwork gained notoriety and became highly sought after by collectors, with some pieces selling for thousands of dollars. Critics and victims' families were outraged by the commercialisation of his crimes, arguing that his ability to profit from his notoriety was a grotesque mockery of justice.

Throughout his years on death row, Gacy maintained his innocence, even in the face of overwhelming evidence against him. In interviews, he portrayed himself as a victim of a corrupt legal system, claiming that he had been framed by law enforcement and that the bodies found on his property had been planted. He insisted that he was a scapegoat and often pointed to perceived inconsistencies in the investigation to support his claims.

Gacy's denial extended to the victims themselves. He frequently dismissed the victims as runaways or criminals, minimising their lives and suggesting that their deaths were inconsequential. This callous attitude only deepened the anguish of the victims' families, who were forced to endure years of Gacy's public declarations and attempts to rewrite history.

In one particularly infamous interview, Gacy stated, "I never killed anybody," despite having confessed to the murders in detail during his initial interrogation. His shifting narratives and refusal to take responsibility for his actions were consistent with the manipulative and narcissistic tendencies he exhibited throughout his life.

The media's fascination with John Wayne Gacy did not end with his conviction. In fact, his time on death row only heightened public interest in his life and crimes. Journalists, filmmakers, and writers sought to understand the man behind the murders, interviewing him extensively and producing countless articles, documentaries, and books about his case. Gacy, always eager for attention, willingly participated in these efforts, granting interviews and sharing his version of events.

One of the most significant aspects of the media's coverage of Gacy was the focus on his clown persona. The image of Gacy as "The Killer Clown" became a cultural symbol of hidden evil, representing the idea that monsters could lurk behind even the most innocent and benign facades. This narrative was perpetuated by Gacy's own artwork, which often featured clowns, and by the sensationalist tone of many media outlets.

While some argued that the media's coverage sensationalised Gacy's crimes and gave him a platform he did not deserve, others believed that it served as an important reminder of the dangers of complacency and the need for vigilance in identifying predatory behaviour.

Like many death row inmates, Gacy spent years appealing his conviction and sentence, utilising every legal avenue available to him. His lawyers argued that he had not received a fair trial, pointing to the extensive media coverage of his case and claiming that his defence team had been ineffective. They also raised questions about the validity of the evidence used to convict him, including the methods used to identify the victims' remains.

These appeals resulted in numerous delays in Gacy's execution, frustrating the victims' families and the public, who were eager for justice to be served. However, the appeals process also highlighted important issues within the criminal justice system, including the complexity of capital punishment cases and the ethical debates surrounding the death penalty.

Despite his legal efforts, Gacy's appeals were ultimately unsuccessful. The courts repeatedly upheld his conviction and sentence, affirming that the evidence against him was overwhelming and that his crimes warranted the harshest punishment.

By the early 1990s, Gacy had exhausted all of his legal options, and the date for his execution was finally set. In the weeks leading up to his death, he continued to maintain his innocence, granting interviews in which he reiterated his claims of being framed and criticised the legal system. He also continued to paint, producing works that were sold to collectors and morbidly fascinated fans.

On May 10, 1994, John Wayne Gacy was executed by lethal injection at Stateville Correctional Center in Illinois. In his final hours, he showed no remorse for his crimes, reportedly spending his time reading and eating a final meal of fried chicken, shrimp, French fries, and strawberries. His last words, "Kiss my ass," were a final act of defiance, reflecting his lifelong refusal to take responsibility for his actions.

Gacy's execution was met with a mix of relief and closure for the victims' families, who had waited years for justice, and broader societal reflection on the legacy of his crimes.

The legacy of John Wayne Gacy is a complex and multifaceted one, encompassing not only the horror of his crimes but also the broader societal and cultural impact of his case. Gacy's story has become a cautionary tale about the dangers of trusting appearances, the failures of the criminal justice system, and the enduring scars left by violence.

1. **A Cautionary Tale**

Gacy's ability to live a double life as a respected businessman and community member while committing unspeakable atrocities highlighted the importance of vigilance in identifying predatory behaviour. His case underscored the idea that evil often hides in plain sight and that predators can be master manipulators who exploit societal blind spots to evade detection.

2. **Impact on Criminal Justice**

Gacy's crimes also exposed significant shortcomings in the criminal justice system. Many of his victims were dismissed as runaways, and the lack of communication between police departments allowed Gacy to continue his spree for years. His case led to calls for improved handling of missing persons cases, better communication between jurisdictions, and greater accountability in law enforcement investigations.

3. **Cultural Fascination**

The media's portrayal of Gacy as "The Killer Clown" cemented his status as one of the most infamous serial killers in history. His story has been the subject of countless books, documentaries, and films, reflecting society's morbid fascination with true crime and the psychology of killers. While this attention has helped to raise awareness about the dangers of unchecked predators, it has also sparked debates about the ethics of sensationalising such cases.

4. **The Victims' Voices**

Despite the focus on Gacy, many have argued that the victims' voices should be prioritised in discussions of his legacy. The young men and boys who lost their lives were more than just statistics—they were individuals with hopes, dreams, and families who loved them. Efforts to memorialise the victims and honour their lives have become an important part of the conversation surrounding Gacy's crimes.

3
BTK – The Hidden Face of Evil

Dennis Rader, better known by the chilling acronym BTK—"Bind, Torture, Kill"—was a man of disturbing contradictions. For over three decades, he led a seemingly ordinary life in Wichita, Kansas, serving as a devoted husband, father, church president, and even a trusted compliance officer in his community. But beneath this façade of normalcy lay a calculated and remorseless predator who stalked, tortured, and murdered ten victims between 1974 and 1991.

What makes BTK's story so unnerving is not just the horror of his crimes, but the duality of his existence. By day, Rader blended seamlessly into his suburban surroundings, garnering trust and respect from those around him. By night, he meticulously planned his attacks, deriving pleasure from his victims' suffering and relishing the control he wielded over their lives. Rader's need for domination extended beyond his physical crimes—he taunted law enforcement and the media with a series of cryptic letters and poems, turning his spree into a twisted game that kept an entire community on edge for decades.

This chapter delves into the life and crimes of Dennis Rader, tracing the evolution of a man who epitomised the hidden darkness that can exist behind the most mundane appearances. From his early life and the development of his twisted fantasies, to the meticulous planning of his murders and his eventual capture, we will explore how Rader maintained his dual identity and eluded justice for so long. In examining the mind and methods of BTK, we confront one of the most chilling truths about human nature: monsters don't always look like monsters. Sometimes, they sit quietly among us, wearing the mask of normalcy.

Early Life and Formative Years

Dennis Lynn Rader, later known as the infamous BTK killer—short for "Bind, Torture, Kill"—was born on **March 9, 1945**, in Pittsburg, Kansas. He was the first of four sons born to William and Dorothea Rader, a middle-class couple who lived in the quiet, rural Midwest. The Raders moved to Wichita, Kansas, soon after Dennis's birth, settling in the suburb of Park City. To the outside world, Dennis's childhood appeared typical for the time, marked by the same values of hard work, family loyalty, and religious observance that shaped many working-class American families in the mid-20th century. However, as with many future killers, the cracks in this idyllic exterior began to show even in his formative years.

While Rader's upbringing did not involve overt abuse or extreme hardship, it was far from nurturing. His father, William, worked long hours as a Kansas Gas and Electric employee, while his mother, Dorothea, was busy with various clerical jobs. Both parents were described as distant, prioritising work and practicality over emotional engagement. Although Rader later claimed to have loved and respected his parents, he also recalled feeling neglected and overshadowed as a child, particularly by his mother, whom he craved attention from but rarely received it.

This lack of emotional warmth from his parents may have played a significant role in Rader's later development. Research on attachment theory suggests that children who feel emotionally neglected often struggle with feelings of inadequacy and low self-esteem. To cope, some develop maladaptive behaviours such as withdrawing emotionally or seeking control over others. For Rader, the seeds of his need for domination, control, and recognition may have been planted during these early years of emotional neglect.

Even as a child, Dennis Rader exhibited behaviours that hinted at his darker tendencies. One of the most telling signs of his future pathology was his fascination with control, pain, and domination. From a young age, Rader admitted to having violent fantasies, which he later referred to as his "factor X." This term, which he used frequently in his writings, referred to the internal drive he believed compelled him to kill—a force he claimed he could not control or understand.

Rader's violent fantasies often centred on women. He imagined scenarios where he could bind and torture them, deriving a sense of pleasure from the thought of having absolute control over another person. By his early teens, these fantasies had developed into more structured daydreams, many of which he would later attempt to recreate during his killings. While many adolescents experience some degree of curiosity about power and control, Rader's fantasies were far from typical. They were not fleeting or exploratory but deeply rooted in his psyche, growing more vivid and detailed as he aged.

Rader's early years also included one of the most consistent warning signs among future serial killers: cruelty to animals. He later admitted to torturing and killing small animals as a child, acts he found both thrilling and empowering. This behaviour is part of what psychologists refer to as the "Macdonald Triad," a set of childhood behaviours—including animal cruelty, fire-setting, and persistent bed-wetting—that are sometimes linked to violent tendencies later in life. For Rader, the act of harming animals provided him with an early outlet for his need to dominate and inflict suffering, giving him a sense of power he lacked in his everyday life.

Another key characteristic of Rader's personality that emerged during his formative years was his intense need for control and recognition. As a child, Rader felt invisible, overlooked by both his parents and his peers. This sense of invisibility fuelled a deep resentment, particularly toward those who seemed to have the attention or power he craved. Over time, this resentment evolved into a desire to assert dominance over others as a way of compensating for his feelings of inadequacy.

Control became a recurring theme in Rader's life. He sought it in small, everyday ways, such as organising his possessions meticulously or exerting authority over his younger siblings. This need for control would later manifest in more disturbing ways, particularly in his treatment of his victims, whom he bound and tortured to satisfy his compulsion to dominate.

Rader also had a strong desire for recognition, though he struggled to achieve it in traditional ways. In school, he was an average student, neither excelling academically nor standing out in extracurricular activities. His classmates described him as quiet and unremarkable, someone who blended into the background. While this anonymity may have protected him from scrutiny as an adult, it deeply frustrated him as a child. Rader longed to be seen, admired, and respected, but he lacked the social skills or talents to achieve this through positive means.

During his teenage years, Rader's darker tendencies continued to develop, though they remained hidden beneath a seemingly normal exterior. He participated in typical adolescent activities, such as attending church and working part-time jobs, but he also began engaging in more secretive and disturbing behaviours. For example, he admitted to engaging in voyeurism, spying on women through their windows and fantasising about tying them up. This practice, which he referred to as "trolling," became a precursor to his later stalking and targeting of victims.

Rader also experimented with autoerotic asphyxiation and other forms of self-bondage during this time. He later described how he would bind himself with ropes or belts, imagining himself as both the victim and the perpetrator in his fantasies. These acts provided him with a sense of control and sexual gratification, reinforcing the connection between violence and pleasure in his mind.

Despite these troubling behaviours, Rader's outward life remained relatively normal. He graduated from Wichita Heights High School in 1963 and briefly attended Kansas Wesleyan University, though he struggled academically and eventually dropped out. His inability to succeed in higher education further fuelled his feelings of inadequacy, though he continued to mask these emotions with a calm and unassuming demeanour.

One of the most striking contradictions in Rader's life was his strong connection to religion, even during his early years. Raised in a Lutheran household, Rader attended church regularly and was heavily influenced by the teachings of Christianity. He often portrayed himself as a devout believer, and his religious upbringing instilled in him a sense of moral superiority that he carried into adulthood.

However, Rader's interpretation of religion was deeply skewed. While he outwardly adhered to Christian values, he used his faith as a tool to justify and compartmentalise his darker impulses. He saw himself as a complex figure, someone who could commit heinous acts while still considering himself a man of faith. This ability to rationalise his actions became a cornerstone of his psychological makeup, allowing him to live a double life without apparent conflict.

By the time Dennis Rader reached adulthood, the foundations for his future crimes were firmly in place. His childhood and adolescence were marked by emotional neglect, a desperate need for control, and deeply ingrained fantasies of domination and violence. While he appeared to be an average young man, his mind was a battleground of conflicting impulses, with his desire for recognition and power growing stronger by the day.

As he transitioned into adulthood, Rader's ability to mask his darker side became one of his most powerful tools. He learned how to present himself as a polite, hardworking individual while keeping his violent fantasies hidden from those around him. This duality would define the rest of his life, enabling him to commit unspeakable acts while maintaining the facade of an ordinary man.

The Making of a Double Life

Dennis Rader's ability to live a double life remains one of the most chilling aspects of his story. For decades, he seamlessly alternated between two identities: a devoted husband, father, and community leader, and the cold-blooded murderer who called himself BTK—"Bind, Torture, Kill." This duality wasn't something Rader stumbled upon; it was meticulously constructed over years. Through calculated decisions, he created a facade so convincing that even those closest to him were unable to see the monster lurking beneath.

The making of Rader's double life began in his young adulthood and was refined through his professional life, relationships, and community involvement. While his public persona gained admiration and trust, his private world was one of twisted fantasies and calculated violence. Understanding how he constructed and maintained this double life sheds light on his psychology and the systems of manipulation he used to evade detection for so long.

In 1971, Dennis Rader married Paula Dietz, a woman from Park City, Kansas, who worked as a bookkeeper. Their marriage marked a turning point in Rader's life, giving him a stable domestic foundation that would serve as the cornerstone of his double life. Paula described Rader as a kind and responsible man, someone who seemed dedicated to his family and home life. Together, they would go on to have two children, a son and a daughter, cementing the image of Rader as a devoted husband and father.

Rader took great care to nurture this outward image. He participated in family activities, attended church regularly, and helped with household chores. To Paula and the children, Rader was a steady and dependable presence, someone they could rely on. He built a reputation as a hard worker and a loving father who cherished family time. His ability to maintain this facade is particularly chilling, as it meant he was able to commit brutal murders while continuing to lead a seemingly ordinary domestic life.

The stability provided by his marriage gave Rader the freedom to pursue his dark impulses in secret. While his family saw him as a provider and protector, Rader compartmentalised his predatory desires, ensuring that his wife and children never suspected the horrors he was capable of. This compartmentalisation was key to his double life: he was able to mask his criminal activities behind the veneer of a typical suburban existence.

Before settling down with Paula, Rader spent four years in the U.S. Air Force, serving from 1966 to 1970. His time in the military played a significant role in shaping his double life, as it provided him with the discipline, structure, and skills he would later use to plan and execute his crimes.

During his military service, Rader learned how to follow orders, maintain a low profile, and adapt to various situations—traits that would become invaluable in his later criminal activities. He also developed an appreciation for routine and meticulous planning, qualities that defined both his public persona and his crimes. While stationed overseas, Rader reportedly engaged in voyeuristic behaviour, a precursor to the stalking and surveillance techniques he would later use to target his victims.

Despite his troubling tendencies, Rader's time in the military earned him respect and a clean record. He returned to civilian life with a sense of accomplishment and the tools he needed to maintain the illusion of normalcy.

Religion played a central role in Rader's double life, providing him with both a moral shield and a platform for public trust. Raised in a Lutheran household, Rader was an active member of Christ Lutheran Church in Park City. Over the years, he became a respected figure within the congregation, serving as president of the church council and participating in community events.

Rader's involvement in the church reinforced his image as a moral and upstanding citizen. He used his religious affiliation to gain the trust of those around him, positioning himself as a man of faith who upheld Christian values. This outward piety served as a stark contrast to his private actions, making it nearly impossible for others to suspect him of wrongdoing.

Rader's ability to reconcile his faith with his crimes speaks to the depth of his compartmentalisation. He claimed to be a devout Christian, yet he derived pleasure from acts of violence and domination. This duality was not just a means of deception; it was a core part of his identity. Rader saw himself as a complex figure, someone who could commit heinous acts while maintaining a moral facade.

Rader's professional life also contributed to his double life, as he gravitated toward roles that gave him authority and control over others. After a brief stint at Kansas Wesleyan University, Rader worked various jobs before settling into a position as a compliance officer in Park City. In this role, he was responsible for enforcing local ordinances, such as property maintenance and pet control.

As a compliance officer, Rader was known for his strict enforcement of the rules. Neighbours described him as a stickler for regulations, someone who would issue citations for minor infractions and take pleasure in asserting his authority. His job allowed him to exercise control over others, feeding into his desire for power and domination.

Rader's career also reinforced his public image as a responsible and trustworthy member of the community. To those who interacted with him professionally, he was simply doing his job—firm but fair.

This perception allowed him to maintain his facade, even as his crimes escalated.

While Rader's public life flourished, his criminal persona continued to evolve in the shadows. By the early 1970s, he had begun developing a systematic approach to targeting and killing his victims. He referred to this process as "trolling," a term he used to describe the act of stalking potential victims and studying their routines.

Rader's methodical nature was evident in every aspect of his crimes. He kept detailed notes about his victims, including their schedules, habits, and vulnerabilities. He often spent weeks or even months observing his targets, ensuring that he knew exactly when and how to strike. This level of planning allowed him to execute his murders with precision, leaving little room for error.

Rader's ability to separate his criminal activities from his public life was a testament to his meticulousness. He carried out his murders with the same level of discipline and organisation that defined his professional and personal life, ensuring that there were no visible connections between the two.

One of the most defining aspects of Rader's double life was his need for recognition. While he was able to keep his crimes hidden from those around him, he craved acknowledgment for his actions. This desire led him to create the BTK persona, a name that encapsulated his modus operandi: bind, torture, kill.

Rader's decision to taunt law enforcement and the media with letters, poems, and detailed accounts of his crimes was both a power play and a cry for attention. He wanted the world to know about BTK, to fear him and respect his intelligence. His communications often included cryptic messages and puzzles, designed to showcase his cunning and keep investigators guessing.

The creation of the BTK persona was a key component of Rader's double life. It allowed him to assert control over the narrative of his crimes, ensuring that he remained in the spotlight. At the same time, it reinforced the divide between his public and private identities, as no one suspected that the mild-mannered family man was the same person as the notorious BTK killer.

Rader's ability to maintain his double life for decades was a result of his careful planning, psychological compartmentalisation, and the trust he had built within his community. He took great care to ensure that his public life remained separate from his criminal activities, creating an impenetrable facade that shielded him from suspicion.

To his family, Rader was a loving husband and father who enjoyed camping trips, barbecues, and church functions. To his neighbours, he was a helpful and friendly man who cared about the well-being of the community. To his colleagues, he was a hardworking and reliable employee who took pride in his work.

This carefully constructed image allowed Rader to continue his killing spree without detection, even as he escalated his crimes. It also highlighted the chilling reality of his duality: the same man who helped his children with their homework and led church meetings was capable of unspeakable acts of violence.

Despite his meticulousness, cracks in Rader's facade began to emerge over time. His strict enforcement of local ordinances earned him a reputation as overly authoritarian, with some neighbours describing him as petty and power-hungry. These complaints, while minor, hinted at the controlling and domineering personality that defined his private life.

In addition, Rader's decision to resurface as BTK in 2004 after years of silence ultimately led to his downfall. His desire for recognition and control over the narrative of his crimes outweighed his caution, exposing him to the scrutiny that would eventually unravel his double life.

The Birth of BTK

The name "BTK"—standing for Bind, Torture, Kill—is a chilling acronym that Dennis Rader himself crafted, embodying the gruesome methodology of his murders. The origins of BTK trace back to the early 1970s, when Rader committed his first murders and began to shape the persona that would later haunt Wichita, Kansas, for decades. This chapter examines the progression of Rader's criminal behaviour, from his early fantasies to the horrifying reality of his first killings, and how the BTK identity was born.

Before Dennis Rader became BTK, his violent tendencies and deviant fantasies had already begun to take form. As a child, Rader admitted to fantasising about bondage and control. He would imagine tying up women and dominating them, finding satisfaction in these thoughts of absolute power. These fantasies developed further during his adolescence, becoming increasingly vivid and sexualised. By his teenage years, Rader was engaging in voyeurism and practising self-bondage, behaviours that offered him a sense of control and fed his escalating fantasies.

The term "factor X" was one Rader later used to describe what he believed drove him to kill. He claimed this internal force compelled him to act on his fantasies, describing it as something he couldn't fully understand or control. Whether this "factor X" was a psychological rationalisation for his behaviour or a manifestation of his narcissism, it reflects his deep need to justify his actions to himself and others. These fantasies were the foundation for the predator he would become.

By the early 1970s, Rader had developed what he referred to as "trolling." This was the process of stalking potential victims, observing their habits, and selecting targets who fit the profile of his fantasies. For Rader, trolling was not just preparation—it was part of the thrill. He relished the act of surveillance, the feeling of power it gave him to watch and study people without their knowledge.

Rader's trolling activities became increasingly methodical. He would drive around Wichita, looking for women who caught his eye. Once he identified a potential target, he would take note of their daily routines, their homes, and any vulnerabilities he could exploit. This meticulous planning became a hallmark of his crimes, allowing him to strike with precision and avoid detection.

The birth of BTK as an active killer came on January 15, 1974, when Rader committed his first murders. The Otero family—a husband, wife, and two of their children—were his initial victims. This brutal crime marked the beginning of Rader's reign of terror in Wichita and introduced his chilling modus operandi to the world.

Rader had selected the Otero family after noticing Julie Otero, the mother, during one of his trolling sessions. She fit the profile of the women in his fantasies: attractive, vulnerable, and within reach. However, Rader did not initially plan to kill the entire family. His original intent was to bind and dominate Julie, deriving pleasure from her fear and helplessness.

On the morning of January 15, Rader broke into the Otero home armed with a gun and a plan. Inside, he found not just Julie but her husband, Joseph, and two of their children, 11-year-old Joseph Jr. and 9-year-old Josephine. Despite the unexpected presence of the entire family, Rader adapted his plan and used his gun to gain control, forcing them into submission. Over the next several hours, he methodically bound, tortured, and killed each member of the family.

Joseph Otero was strangled to death first, followed by his wife, Julie. Rader then turned his attention to the children. He strangled Joseph Jr. with a plastic bag and took special pleasure in tormenting Josephine, whom he hung in the basement in a manner that fulfilled his deviant fantasies. The gruesome details of the Otero murders, later revealed by Rader himself, shocked even seasoned investigators.

The discovery of the Otero family's bodies sent shockwaves through Wichita. The community, which had previously been considered safe and peaceful, was suddenly gripped by fear. The brutality of the murders and the lack of any clear motive or suspect left residents and law enforcement alike searching for answers.

For Rader, the Otero murders were a success. He had fulfilled his fantasies and experienced the rush of power and control that came with dominating and killing his victims. However, the experience also left him wanting more. The satisfaction he derived from the murders was fleeting, and he quickly began to plan his next attack.

After the Otero murders, Rader refined his methods and began to develop the distinct modus operandi that would define BTK. His approach was methodical, calculated, and ritualistic, designed to maximise his control over his victims and the pleasure he derived from their suffering.

Selection of Victims:
Rader typically chose women who were vulnerable and fit the profile of his fantasies. He preferred victims who lived alone or were isolated, making it easier for him to gain control without interference. He would stalk his targets for weeks, learning their routines and identifying opportunities to strike.

The Break-In:
Rader often gained access to his victims' homes through forced entry or by posing as someone in need of help. Once inside, he used his calm demeanour and weapons to gain control, ensuring his victims complied with his demands.

Binding and Torture:

As his name suggests, binding was a central element of Rader's crimes. He used ropes, cords, and other materials to restrain his victims, often tying them in intricate and humiliating positions. This act was deeply connected to his fantasies, providing him with a sense of domination and power.

Murder:
Rader's preferred method of killing was strangulation, which he saw as intimate and personal. He often used ligatures, tightening them slowly to prolong his victims' suffering. In some cases, he suffocated his victims with plastic bags or other materials, relishing the control he had over their lives.

Souvenirs and Documentation:
After each murder, Rader would take souvenirs from his victims, such as clothing, jewellery, or personal items. These objects served as trophies, allowing him to relive his crimes. He also documented his killings through notes, drawings, and photographs, creating a detailed record of his activities.

Following the Otero murders, Rader began to shape his public persona as BTK. In October 1974, he sent his first letter to The Wichita Eagle, taking credit for the Otero murders and providing specific details that only the killer could know. In this letter, Rader introduced the name BTK, which he claimed encapsulated his methods: Bind, Torture, Kill.

The letter was chilling in its tone and content. Rader described the murders in graphic detail, taunting both the media and law enforcement. He expressed frustration that his crimes had not received the attention he believed they deserved, demanding recognition for his actions. This need for validation became a defining characteristic of BTK, as Rader continued to communicate with the media and police throughout his killing spree.

By adopting the name BTK, Rader created a persona that was separate from his public identity as Dennis Rader. This allowed him to compartmentalise his actions, maintaining his facade as a devoted husband, father, and church leader while embracing his darker impulses in secret. The BTK persona was not just a mask—it was a manifestation of Rader's narcissism and his desire for control, recognition, and immortality.

Over the next several years, Rader continued his killing spree, targeting women and, in some cases, their families. Each murder was meticulously planned and executed, showcasing the methods he had developed during the Otero murders. Some of his most notable victims during this period included:

- **Kathryn Bright (April 4, 1974):** Rader broke into her home and ambushed her and her brother, Kevin. Although Kevin survived after being shot, Kathryn was bound and stabbed to death.

- **Shirley Vian (March 17, 1977):** Rader targeted Shirley after stalking her for weeks. He bound her with ropes and strangled her while her young children were locked in another room.

- **Nancy Fox (December 8, 1977):** Nancy was one of Rader's most carefully planned murders. He stalked her for weeks before breaking into her home, binding her, and strangling her.

Each murder reinforced Rader's sense of power and control, feeding the fantasies that drove him. At the same time, his communications with the media and police escalated, as he sought to cement his identity as BTK in the public consciousness.

Taunting the Police and Media

Dennis Rader, known as BTK (Bind, Torture, Kill), was not only a murderer but a manipulator who thrived on the attention his crimes garnered. Between 1974 and his eventual capture in 2005, Rader went beyond the acts of violence he committed, engaging in a psychological game with law enforcement and the media. By sending letters, poems, and detailed accounts of his crimes, he ensured that the name BTK became synonymous with terror in Wichita, Kansas. This chapter delves into Rader's obsession with recognition, his communications with police and media, and the role his taunting played in his eventual capture.

Rader's need for recognition became evident soon after his first murders. Following the brutal slayings of the Otero family in January 1974, the crime initially baffled investigators. There were no immediate leads or suspects, and the case threatened to fade from public consciousness. Rader, however, refused to let that happen. He wanted credit for the killings and to establish himself as a figure of fear. His first known communication came in **October 1974**, when he sent a letter to *The Wichita Eagle-Beacon*, claiming responsibility for the Otero murders.

The letter was chilling in both tone and content. It included specific details about the crime scene that only the killer could have known, such as the positions of the bodies and the methods used to kill each victim. Rader's intention was clear: to leave no doubt that he was the perpetrator. The letter also contained a critical moment in the creation of his public persona—he introduced himself as BTK, explaining that the acronym stood for "Bind, Torture, Kill," a concise summary of his modus operandi.

The effect of the letter was immediate. The public, which had largely moved on from the Otero murders, was gripped by fear. The letter confirmed that a sadistic killer was operating in their midst and that he was both methodical and arrogant enough to taunt the authorities. For Rader, the letter was a success. It established his identity as BTK and ensured that his crimes would remain in the spotlight.

Rader's decision to engage with the police and media was not a mere whim—it was deeply rooted in his psychology. His letters and taunts served multiple purposes:

1. **Recognition and Validation:**

Rader's primary motivation was to ensure that his crimes were acknowledged. He wanted the world to know that BTK was a cunning, dangerous predator who could not be caught. By controlling the narrative, he satisfied his need for attention and reinforced his sense of superiority.

2. **Power and Control:**

Taunting law enforcement gave Rader a sense of power. He enjoyed watching the police scramble to piece together his cryptic clues, knowing that he held all the answers. This psychological game of cat-and-mouse was, in many ways, an extension of the control he exerted over his victims.

3. **Feeding His Ego:**

Rader's communications were often laced with narcissism. He portrayed himself as an intelligent and sophisticated killer, frequently mocking the police for their inability to catch him. This inflated sense of self-importance drove much of his behaviour, both in his crimes and in his taunts.

4. **Rekindling the Thrill:**

Rader often referred to the "high" he experienced during his killings. After the act, however, that thrill would fade, leaving him restless and dissatisfied. By sending letters and poems, he could relive his crimes and recapture the excitement.

Rader's communications were varied, ranging from detailed letters to bizarre poems. Each piece served as a window into his mind, revealing his arrogance, need for attention, and disturbing sense of humour.

In December 1977, after murdering Nancy Fox, Rader sent a letter to *The Wichita Eagle* providing details of the crime. The letter was short but direct, written in a cold and detached tone. He described the methods he used to kill Fox, leaving no doubt that he was the perpetrator. The inclusion of specific details once again ensured that law enforcement and the media would take his claims seriously.

Rader also made a chilling phone call to police following Fox's murder, during which he directed them to her address. This call, recorded and later played during his trial, captured the calm and emotionless voice of a man who took pleasure in orchestrating chaos.

Rader occasionally expressed his twisted thoughts through poetry. One of his most infamous poems, "Oh Death to Nancy," was a disturbing ode to Nancy Fox, whom he had murdered. The poem blended mockery, fantasy, and self-glorification, showcasing his warped mindset. Writing these poems allowed Rader to personalise his crimes and maintain his psychological connection to his victims.

In 1978, Rader sent a particularly cryptic letter to KAKE-TV, a local television station in Wichita. The letter included a puzzle, which he described as a "coded message" that would reveal his identity. The puzzle was never solved, but it reinforced Rader's desire to portray himself as an intellectual adversary to law enforcement.

After a hiatus of more than a decade, Rader re-emerged in 2004. His desire for recognition, which had been dormant, was reignited when a local newspaper ran a feature on the 30th anniversary of the Otero murders, speculating that BTK might still be at large. This article acted as a trigger for Rader, who felt the need to reclaim the spotlight.

Rader began sending a new series of letters, packages, and communications, reintroducing BTK to the public. These communications included:

- A letter with detailed accounts of his previous murders.

- A chapter list for a "BTK Story" autobiography, complete with sarcastic titles for each section of his crimes.

- A package containing a Barbie doll bound in the same way as one of his victims, symbolising his methods.

- A word search puzzle with hidden references to his crimes.

Each communication served to taunt law enforcement and remind the public that BTK was still active, though his killing spree had ended years earlier.

The media played a crucial role in Rader's taunting. By publishing his letters and covering his crimes extensively, they provided him with the attention he craved. Rader was acutely aware of how his actions were portrayed in the press and often tailored his communications to maximise their impact. For example, he used language and phrasing designed to provoke fear and intrigue, ensuring that his letters would dominate headlines.

At the same time, the media's involvement was a double-edged sword. While it gave Rader the validation he sought, it also intensified the public pressure on law enforcement to catch him. The increased scrutiny eventually led to the breakthroughs that resulted in his capture.

Rader's taunting posed a significant challenge for law enforcement. His communications provided valuable insights into his psychology and methods, but they also frustrated investigators, who struggled to piece together the cryptic clues he left behind. Despite their best efforts, Rader's careful planning and lack of a clear pattern made him difficult to track.

One of the key turning points in the investigation came in 2004, when Rader sent a floppy disk to the police. The disk contained metadata linking it to the Christ Lutheran Church, where Rader served as president. This crucial mistake allowed investigators to identify Rader as the prime suspect, ultimately leading to his arrest.

Rader's decision to taunt the police and media had far-reaching consequences. On one hand, it ensured that his crimes would be remembered, fulfilling his desire for recognition. On the other hand, it contributed to his downfall, as his need for attention led him to make critical errors.

For the public, Rader's taunting reinforced the image of BTK as a calculated and sadistic killer who enjoyed playing games with his victims and the authorities. His communications added an extra layer of terror to his crimes, as they demonstrated his willingness to manipulate and torment not just his victims but an entire community.

The Continued Killing Spree

Dennis Rader, the BTK killer, escalated his killing spree from the mid-1970s to the early 1990s, preying on unsuspecting victims in Wichita, Kansas. During this period, Rader meticulously planned his attacks, carefully selected his targets, and executed his crimes with a methodical precision that made him both terrifying and elusive. This chapter delves into the details of Rader's continued murders, his psychological motivations, and how he maintained his facade as a model citizen while committing some of the most horrifying crimes in American history.

Rader's modus operandi (MO) during this period followed a clear, chilling pattern. His crimes were not random but carefully planned, reflecting his desire for control and domination. The acronym BTK—"Bind, Torture, Kill"—encapsulated his methods, which involved:

1. **Stalking and Planning:**

Rader would spend weeks, sometimes months, stalking his potential victims. He referred to this process as "trolling." He watched their routines, learned their vulnerabilities, and planned the best time to strike. This stalking phase was not just preparation—it was a source of psychological satisfaction for Rader, as it fed his fantasies of control and power.

2. **Breaking In:**

Rader gained access to his victims' homes through a variety of methods, including forced entry, deception, or ambush. Once inside, he used his calm demeanour and weapons to subdue his victims, often tying them up with ropes or other materials he brought with him.

3. **Binding and Torture:**

The binding of his victims was central to Rader's fantasies. He used ropes, cords, or other items to restrain his victims in humiliating and painful positions. This process allowed him to assert complete control over them, fulfilling his psychological need for domination.

4. **Killing:**

Rader's preferred method of killing was strangulation, as he found it to be intimate and satisfying. He often used ligatures, tightening them slowly to prolong his victims' suffering. In some cases, he used plastic bags to suffocate his victims.

5. **Trophies and Documentation:**

After each murder, Rader took trophies, such as clothing, jewellery, or personal items, to relive the crime later. He also documented his killings through notes, drawings, and photographs, creating a macabre archive of his crimes.

During his continued killing spree, Rader claimed multiple victims. Each murder was marked by his distinctive MO, yet each crime also reflected his adaptability and evolving techniques.

Kathryn Bright (April 4, 1974)

Rader's second known murder occurred just three months after the Otero family killings. He targeted 21-year-old Kathryn Bright, a young woman who lived in Wichita. After stalking her for weeks, Rader broke into her home, expecting to find her alone. However, Kathryn's brother, Kevin, was with her when Rader arrived.

Rader ambushed the siblings, forcing them into separate rooms at gunpoint. He tied up Kevin and attempted to strangle him, but Kevin fought back, managing to free himself despite being shot twice in the head. Rader then turned his attention to Kathryn, binding and stabbing her multiple times. Though Kevin survived and later provided critical details about the attack, Kathryn succumbed to her injuries.

This crime revealed several aspects of Rader's psychology. His rage and loss of control when Kevin resisted demonstrated his need for absolute dominance. Despite this deviation from his plan, Rader viewed the murder as a success, as it reinforced his belief in his ability to adapt and kill under pressure.

Shirley Vian (March 17, 1977)

Three years after Kathryn Bright's murder, Rader struck again, targeting 26-year-old Shirley Vian. Shirley was home with her three children when Rader forced his way into their house. Using a gun, he separated Shirley from her children, locking the terrified kids in the bathroom.

Rader then bound Shirley with ropes and suffocated her with a plastic bag. He later admitted that he left the scene quickly, fearing that someone might have noticed him entering the home. While the children survived, the psychological trauma they endured would last a lifetime.

This murder demonstrated Rader's increasing confidence and boldness. Despite the presence of witnesses, he was willing to take significant risks to satisfy his fantasies. His ability to maintain his composure during such a high-stakes situation further highlights his calculated nature.

Nancy Fox (December 8, 1977)

Nancy Fox, a 25-year-old secretary, became one of Rader's most infamous victims. After stalking her for weeks, he broke into her home and waited for her to return. Once inside, Rader ambushed Nancy, binding and strangling her in her bedroom.

Nancy's murder stood out for two reasons. First, Rader called the police himself afterward to report the crime, providing the address and calmly stating that they would find a body there. This brazen act of taunting law enforcement highlighted his growing arrogance and need for recognition. Second, Rader later wrote a poem, "Oh Death to Nancy," which he sent to the media, further showcasing his desire to control the narrative surrounding his crimes.

The 1980s: An Era of Silence and Speculation

After the murder of 53-year-old Marine Hedge in 1985, Rader seemed to enter a period of relative silence. His killings slowed dramatically, and he avoided direct communication with law enforcement and the media. This lull in activity led many to believe that BTK had disappeared or been incarcerated for unrelated crimes.

Rader, however, was far from inactive. During this time, he continued to stalk potential victims, engaging in voyeurism and other forms of psychological preparation. He also focused on his family and community life, serving as president of his church council and working as a compliance officer in Park City. This period of silence demonstrated Rader's ability to compartmentalise his life, maintaining his public facade while keeping his darker impulses hidden.

The Later Murders

Rader's killing spree officially ended in 1991, though he likely continued to fantasise about committing further murders. His final known victims include:

- **Marine Hedge (April 27, 1985):** Rader strangled the 53-year-old widow in her home before taking her body to a church, where he posed and photographed it in various positions. This act demonstrated his escalating need for control and documentation.

- **Vicki Wegerle (September 16, 1986):** Rader posed as a telephone repairman to gain access to Vicki's home. Once inside, he overpowered her, bound her with ropes, and strangled her. He later took photographs of her body as trophies.

- **Dolores Davis (January 19, 1991):** Rader broke into Dolores's home, tied her up, and strangled her. He disposed of her body in a secluded area, marking the end of his known murders.

While Rader maintained his public facade, his crimes took a psychological toll on both his victims and the Wichita community. Residents lived in fear, knowing that BTK was still out there, waiting to strike again. The randomness of his attacks—targeting women of various ages and backgrounds—only heightened the terror, as no one felt truly safe.

For Rader, the psychological toll manifested as an insatiable need for recognition. As the years went on, he became increasingly frustrated by the lack of attention his crimes received. This frustration would later lead him to resume communication with the media in 2004, ultimately resulting in his capture.

The BTK Hiatus

The term "hiatus" in the context of serial killers often conjures the image of dormancy or a temporary cessation of activity. In the case of Dennis Rader, also known as BTK (Bind, Torture, Kill), his hiatus from killing between 1991 and 2004 was less about dormancy and more about an evolution of his psychological needs. Though Rader's known murders ceased in 1991, his twisted fantasies, desire for control, and need for recognition persisted. During this time, Rader focused on reinforcing his facade as a model citizen, embedding himself deeper into his family life and community, while occasionally engaging in activities that kept his "factor X"—as he referred to his murderous compulsion—alive.

This chapter explores the key events of Rader's hiatus, the factors that contributed to his temporary cessation of murders, his continued psychological torment and need for control, and how his reemergence in 2004 ultimately led to his downfall.

1991: The Final Murder

Rader's final known murder took place on January 19, 1991, when he killed 62-year-old Dolores Davis. Davis, a widow living alone in Park City, Kansas, became Rader's last victim after he had stalked her and observed her routines. Breaking into her home through a sliding glass door, Rader bound and strangled her before disposing of her body under a bridge.

The murder of Davis marked the end of BTK's known killing spree. By this time, Rader had committed 10 murders over the span of nearly two decades. His crimes had terrorised Wichita and its surrounding areas, leaving law enforcement and the public in fear of when—or if—he would strike again. However, after Davis's death, Rader seemingly vanished. BTK went silent, and for years, no one heard from him.

The question of why Dennis Rader stopped killing has puzzled criminologists and law enforcement officials for years. Serial killers rarely stop voluntarily, as their compulsions are often too strong to resist. For Rader, several factors likely contributed to his decision to halt his murderous activities:

1. **Increased Responsibilities**

By 1991, Rader's personal life had evolved. He was raising two children and had taken on more significant responsibilities at home and in his community. His daughter, Kerri, was a teenager, and his son, Brian, was in his early teens. Rader's role as a father became more demanding, and he was deeply involved in family life, attending school events, helping with extracurricular activities, and maintaining the appearance of a devoted husband and parent. Additionally, Rader's professional life required more of his attention. He worked as a compliance officer for Park City, a job that gave him authority over enforcing local ordinances. While the role allowed him to exert control over others—feeding his need for dominance—it also occupied much of his time, leaving less room for the elaborate planning his murders required.

2. **Fear of Being Caught**

By the late 1980s and early 1990s, advancements in forensic science, particularly DNA profiling, were becoming a more significant factor in solving crimes. Rader was aware of these developments and may have feared that his methods of operation would eventually lead to his capture. His careful nature and obsession with control likely played a role in his decision to stop killing, as he wanted to avoid taking unnecessary risks.

3. **Satiation and Fantasy**

Rader often referred to his "factor X"—a self-described compulsion to kill—as the driving force behind his murders. While his crimes fulfilled his fantasies of control and domination, he also maintained an active fantasy life outside of his murders. During his hiatus, Rader continued to relive his past crimes through his trophies, drawings, and written accounts. These activities may have temporarily satisfied his compulsions, reducing his need to act on them physically.

4. **Life Changes**

As Rader aged, his priorities shifted. In the early 1990s, he became more deeply involved in his church, Christ Lutheran Church, where he served as president of the congregation. His leadership role gave him a new outlet for control and attention, allowing him to maintain his facade of respectability. His growing responsibilities at home, work, and church may have provided a temporary substitute for the power he sought through his killings.

Though Rader's known murders ceased in 1991, his activities during the following decade reveal that he was far from inactive. While he managed to suppress his homicidal urges, his need for control, power, and recognition continued to manifest in other ways.

During the hiatus, Rader appeared to lead an ordinary suburban life. He lived with his wife, Paula, and their two children in Park City, maintaining the image of a devoted husband and father. To outsiders, Rader seemed like the epitome of stability and respectability. He participated in family activities, attended church regularly, and took part in community events. His children, unaware of their father's dark side, grew up believing he was a loving and supportive parent.

Rader's ability to compartmentalise his life is one of the most chilling aspects of his personality. While he outwardly fulfilled his familial and social roles, he continued to nurture his fantasies in private. His family had no idea that the man who attended their school plays and church potlucks was the same person who had terrorised their community as BTK.

Rader's job as a compliance officer for Park City provided him with another outlet for his need for control. In this role, he enforced local ordinances, such as property maintenance and pet control.

Neighbours often described him as strict, overzealous, and petty in his enforcement of rules. Some residents viewed him as a bully who enjoyed wielding his authority over others.

This job gave Rader the opportunity to exercise power in a way that mirrored his crimes. While his actions as a compliance officer were not illegal, they reflected the same psychological need for dominance that drove his killings. He derived satisfaction from asserting authority and making others comply with his demands.

Even during his hiatus, Rader remained immersed in the fantasy world he had created as BTK. He continued to revisit his past crimes through trophies, such as stolen items from his victims, and his detailed writings. Rader kept a collection of journals in which he documented his murders, including the planning, execution, and aftermath of each crime. These journals served as a way for him to relive the thrill of his killings without taking new risks.

In addition to his journals, Rader engaged in voyeurism and stalking, activities that allowed him to maintain a connection to his fantasies without committing murder. He would watch women in his community, observing their routines and imagining scenarios in which he could dominate and control them. While these activities did not result in new murders, they kept his "factor X" alive and fed his compulsion.

One of the primary drivers behind Rader's reemergence in 2004 was his frustration with being forgotten. During his hiatus, BTK faded from public consciousness, as law enforcement and the media focused on other crimes. For someone as narcissistic as Rader, this lack of attention was intolerable.

The 30th anniversary of the Otero family murders in 2004 brought BTK back into the spotlight, sparking renewed media interest in the case. This attention acted as a trigger for Rader, reigniting his desire for recognition. He began sending letters to the media and police, reintroducing himself as BTK and taunting law enforcement with cryptic messages. This decision would ultimately lead to his capture, as his need for validation outweighed his caution.

Rader's decision to break his silence in 2004 marked the end of his hiatus and the beginning of his downfall. Over the next year, he sent a series of letters, packages, and messages to the media and police, reigniting fear in the Wichita community. These communications included:

- A letter describing the details of past murders, ensuring the public remembered his crimes.

- A word search puzzle containing references to his crimes and his identity as BTK.

- A package with a Barbie doll bound in the same way as one of his victims.

Rader's biggest mistake came when he sent a floppy disk to the police, believing it could not be traced. Investigators quickly discovered metadata on the disk linking it to Christ Lutheran Church, where Rader served as president. This clue led to Rader's arrest on **February 25, 2005**, ending his reign of terror.

Resurfacing and Capture

Dennis Rader's reemergence as the BTK killer in 2004 was both calculated and reckless, a culmination of years of suppressed desires for recognition and validation. After more than a decade of silence following his last known murder in 1991, Rader's decision to resurface set the stage for his eventual downfall. His reemergence, driven by his insatiable narcissism and need for control, reignited fear in Wichita, Kansas, and challenged law enforcement to confront a long-dormant case that had haunted the community for decades. This chapter examines the factors that led to Rader's resurfacing, his taunts and communications with law enforcement, and the investigative breakthroughs that led to his capture in 2005.

By 2004, Dennis Rader was no longer active as a killer, but the BTK persona had never truly disappeared. Over the years, he had retreated into his carefully constructed life as a husband, father, church leader, and compliance officer. However, the absence of attention to his crimes during his 13-year hiatus gnawed at him. Rader had always craved validation for his actions, seeing his murders as achievements that deserved recognition. His choice to stay silent had shielded him from detection, but it also left him feeling invisible, a fate he could not tolerate.

The spark for Rader's reemergence came when a local newspaper ran a story marking the 30th anniversary of the Otero family murders in January 2004. The article speculated about whether BTK could still be alive and whether he might ever be caught. For Rader, this was an irresistible opportunity. He saw the renewed media interest as a chance to reclaim the spotlight, to remind the world that BTK was still out there. It was the validation he had been craving, and he could not resist the temptation to respond.

In **March 2004**, Rader sent his first communication in over a decade to *The Wichita Eagle*, reigniting terror in the Wichita community. The letter included a photocopy of Vicki Wegerle's driver's license, a chilling piece of evidence Rader had taken as a trophy when he murdered her in 1986. This letter not only confirmed that BTK was still alive but also proved that the person claiming to be BTK was the real killer.

The letter also contained a series of taunts and cryptic clues, consistent with Rader's earlier communications in the 1970s and 1980s. His tone was self-assured and arrogant, demonstrating his belief that he was still in control. The communication had the desired effect: it reignited public fear and brought BTK back into the media spotlight. For Rader, this was the beginning of his return to prominence.

Over the next year, Rader engaged in a calculated campaign of communication with the media and law enforcement. His letters, packages, and taunts became increasingly bold, revealing his need to assert control over the narrative and keep his identity as BTK at the forefront of public consciousness. Some of the most notable communications during this period include:

1. The Word Puzzle

In May 2004, Rader sent a letter to KAKE-TV, a local television station, containing a word puzzle. The puzzle included hidden references to his crimes and his identity as BTK. While the puzzle itself did not provide any direct clues about his identity, it served to remind the police and the public of his intelligence and his ability to toy with investigators.

2. The Barbie Doll Package

In December 2004, Rader sent a package to a local park containing a bound Barbie doll. The doll was posed to resemble one of his victims, symbolising the binding and torture that had defined his modus operandi. This gruesome gesture was both a taunt and a demonstration of his fixation on his past crimes.

3. The "BTK Story" Autobiography

In January 2005, Rader sent a package to KSAS-TV containing a list of chapters for a fictional autobiography titled "The BTK Story." The chapter titles were laced with sarcasm and dark humour, including entries such as "A Serial Killer Is Born" and "The Final Curtain Call." This document revealed Rader's narcissism and his desire to shape the narrative of his life and crimes.

While Rader's communications demonstrated his cunning and confidence, they also revealed his overconfidence, which ultimately became his downfall. In February 2005, Rader made a critical mistake when he sent a floppy disk to the police. The disk, which contained a document taunting investigators, also held metadata linking it to a computer at Christ Lutheran Church in Park City, Kansas, where Rader served as president of the congregation.

The metadata revealed that the document had been created by someone named "Dennis." This was a significant breakthrough for investigators, who had already been narrowing their list of suspects. The connection to the church allowed law enforcement to identify Dennis Rader as a potential suspect and begin surveilling him.

With Dennis Rader identified as a suspect, law enforcement focused on gathering concrete evidence to link him to the BTK murders. Investigators obtained a warrant to test DNA from Rader's daughter, Kerri, by collecting a sample from a Pap smear she had taken during a medical appointment. The DNA sample provided a familial match to evidence from the BTK crime scenes, confirming that Dennis Rader was the killer.

On February 25, 2005, Rader was arrested near his home in Park City. The arrest was swift and uneventful, with Rader offering little resistance. At the time of his arrest, he was 59 years old and had spent decades living a double life. The man who had terrorised Wichita as BTK was finally in custody, and the long, agonising search for the killer was over.

Following his arrest, Rader provided a chilling confession to law enforcement. Over the course of several hours, he calmly detailed each of the murders, describing his methods and motivations with a disturbing lack of emotion. He referred to his victims as "projects" and described his killings as if they were tasks on a to-do list.

Rader's confession revealed the extent of his planning and the depth of his depravity. He explained how he selected his victims, stalked them, and carried out his crimes. He also admitted to keeping trophies and documenting his murders in journals, which he referred to as his "hidey holes" for memories.

One of the most chilling aspects of Rader's confession was his tone. He spoke about his crimes in a matter-of-fact manner, showing no remorse for the lives he had taken or the pain he had caused. For investigators and the public, this lack of empathy underscored the true nature of his personality—a man who thrived on power, control, and recognition.

The arrest of Dennis Rader brought a mix of relief and horror to Wichita. For decades, the community had lived with the fear of BTK, and his capture provided long-overdue closure for the victims' families. However, the revelation that BTK had been living among them as an unassuming family man and church leader shocked residents to their core. Rader's ability to maintain a double life highlighted the chilling reality that predators can often hide in plain sight.

Confession and Trial

The confession and trial of Dennis Rader, the infamous BTK (Bind, Torture, Kill) killer, were pivotal moments in the history of American criminal justice. These proceedings revealed the depth of Rader's depravity, his chilling lack of remorse, and his ability to live a double life for decades. This chapter delves into Rader's detailed confession, the legal strategies employed during his trial, and the societal and emotional impact on the victims' families and the broader public.

Dennis Rader was arrested on February 25, 2005, near his home in Park City, Kansas. After years of eluding law enforcement, Rader was calm and compliant during his arrest, seemingly resigned to his fate. Police transported him to an interrogation room, where he was confronted with the evidence that had led to his capture, including DNA linking him to multiple BTK crime scenes and metadata from the floppy disk he had sent to law enforcement.

Faced with irrefutable evidence, Rader quickly confessed. Over the course of nearly 30 hours of interrogation, he provided a chillingly detailed account of his crimes. His confession included descriptions of each murder, from the planning stages to the aftermath, and he spoke about his motives and methods with a shocking lack of emotion. For investigators, this was the moment when they came face-to-face with the true BTK—an articulate, meticulous, and remorseless killer.

Rader's confession was marked by his calm and matter-of-fact demeanour. He referred to his victims as "projects" and described his killings as if they were tasks on a checklist. This detached tone underscored his lack of empathy and his view of his victims as mere objects to satisfy his twisted fantasies.

Key Elements of Rader's Confession

1. **The Murders**

Rader confessed to all 10 of his known murders, beginning with the Otero family in 1974 and ending with Dolores Davis in 1991. He described each crime in graphic detail, recounting how he stalked his victims, broke into their homes, and carried out his killings. He explained his methods of binding and torturing his victims and admitted to taking trophies, such as jewellery, clothing, and personal items, to relive the crimes.

Each murder was meticulously planned, and Rader revealed how he selected his victims through a process he called "trolling," during which he observed and stalked potential targets. His ability to evade detection for so long was largely due to his careful planning and his ability to blend into his community.

2. **The "Factor X" Excuse**

During his confession, Rader repeatedly referred to "Factor X," a term he used to describe the supposed force or compulsion that drove him to kill. He claimed that this inner drive was beyond his control and likened it to a supernatural force. While this explanation may have been an attempt to deflect responsibility for his actions, it also highlighted his deep narcissism and need to portray himself as unique and extraordinary.

3. **Taunting Law Enforcement**

Rader openly admitted to sending letters, poems, and other communications to the media and police. He explained that these taunts were intended to assert his dominance and keep his crimes in the public eye. His overconfidence and desire for recognition ultimately led to his downfall, as the floppy disk he sent in 2005 provided investigators with the evidence needed to identify and arrest him.

4. **The Double Life**

Perhaps the most disturbing aspect of Rader's confession was his ability to maintain a double life. He described how he balanced his role as a family man, church leader, and community member with his secret life as a serial killer. His ability to compartmentalise his actions allowed him to evade suspicion for decades, even from those closest to him.

Following his confession, Rader was charged with 10 counts of first-degree murder. The legal proceedings against him posed several challenges for both the prosecution and the defence.

The prosecution's primary goal was to ensure that Rader was held accountable for his crimes and received the maximum sentence under Kansas law. Since Kansas reinstated the death penalty in 1994, and Rader's last known murder occurred in 1991, the death penalty was not applicable in his case. Instead, the prosecution sought 10 consecutive life sentences without the possibility of parole.

To build their case, prosecutors relied heavily on Rader's confession, which provided detailed accounts of each murder. They also presented forensic evidence, including DNA from multiple crime scenes, and testimonies from law enforcement officials who had worked on the case for decades.

Rader's defence team faced an uphill battle, as his confession and the overwhelming evidence left little room for doubt about his guilt. Their primary focus was on ensuring that Rader received a fair trial and avoiding any procedural errors that could lead to appeals.

The defence also considered raising questions about Rader's mental state, as his lack of remorse and bizarre explanations (such as "Factor X") suggested possible psychological disorders. However, Rader was deemed competent to stand trial, and no insanity defence was pursued.

Dennis Rader's trial officially began on **June 27, 2005**, in Sedgwick County District Court. Unlike many high-profile trials, Rader chose to waive his right to a jury trial and entered a guilty plea to all 10 charges of first-degree murder. This decision spared the victims' families the ordeal of a lengthy trial and ensured that Rader's guilt was formally acknowledged in court.

Despite his guilty plea, the trial was not without drama. The court proceedings included victim impact statements, detailed accounts of the murders, and a chilling allocution from Rader himself.

As part of his guilty plea, Rader was required to provide an allocution—a formal statement admitting to his crimes and explaining his actions. Over the course of several hours, Rader described each murder in excruciating detail, from the initial stalking phase to the moment of the killings. He spoke with a disturbing lack of emotion, as if recounting mundane tasks.

Rader's allocution revealed the meticulous planning behind his murders and his twisted sense of pride in his crimes. He referred to his victims by name but showed no remorse, instead focusing on the logistics of his actions. For the victims' families and the public, his words were both horrifying and dehumanising.

One of the most powerful moments of the trial came when the families of Rader's victims delivered impact statements. These statements allowed the families to share their pain and grief, giving a voice to the lives that Rader had so callously taken.

The impact statements were emotional and heart-wrenching, as family members recounted their memories of the victims and the devastating effects of their loss. Many expressed anger and disbelief at Rader's ability to live a normal life while committing such heinous acts. Others shared their hope that justice would bring some measure of closure.

Rader showed little reaction during the impact statements, maintaining his stoic demeanour and refusing to engage with the emotions of the families. This lack of empathy further underscored his sociopathic tendencies.

On August 18, 2005, Dennis Rader was sentenced to 10 consecutive life sentences without the possibility of parole. The judge, Gregory Waller, described Rader's crimes as "horrific beyond imagination" and condemned him as a man without a soul. The sentence ensured that Rader would spend the rest of his life in prison, unable to harm anyone else.

The sentencing brought a sense of relief to the victims' families and the Wichita community, who had lived in fear of BTK for decades. While no punishment could undo the damage Rader had caused, his imprisonment provided a measure of justice and closure.

The trial of Dennis Rader captivated the nation, drawing widespread media attention and sparking debates about the psychology of serial killers, the role of law enforcement, and the impact of media coverage on criminal cases. Rader's confession and trial revealed the depth of his depravity and the chilling reality of his double life, leaving an indelible mark on the public consciousness.

Legacy and Lessons: Understanding the Impact of BTK

The legacy of Dennis Rader, better known as BTK (Bind, Torture, Kill), extends far beyond the heinous crimes he committed. His ability to live a double life as a family man and respected community member while secretly carrying out a spree of torture and murder shocked not only his hometown of Wichita, Kansas, but also the broader world. BTK's story forces society to confront the complexities of human psychology, the vulnerabilities of criminal justice systems, and the pervasive impact of his actions on victims, their families, and entire communities.

This chapter examines Rader's lasting legacy, the lessons learned from his crimes and capture, and the broader implications of his case in fields such as criminology, law enforcement, psychology, and public awareness.

Dennis Rader's name will forever be synonymous with terror. His moniker, BTK, reflects his signature modus operandi—binding, torturing, and killing his victims in a way that maximised their suffering and his sense of control. Between 1974 and 1991, Rader murdered 10 people, including children, leaving a trail of fear and devastation in his wake.

1. The Psychological Toll on Wichita

Rader's reign of terror deeply affected the Wichita community. For decades, residents lived with the fear that BTK could strike again. The randomness of his attacks, combined with his ability to evade capture, left people feeling vulnerable and mistrustful. Parents worried about their children, women feared being alone in their homes, and a sense of safety was shattered.

Even after his arrest in 2005, the psychological scars remained. The revelation that Rader had lived among them as a seemingly normal man—a husband, father, church leader, and compliance officer—heightened the sense of betrayal and unease. His ability to blend into the community reinforced the chilling reality that predators can hide in plain sight.

2. The Cultural Symbol of BTK

Rader's crimes and persona have left an indelible mark on popular culture. The image of BTK as a calculated, sadistic killer who taunted police and the media has inspired books, documentaries, and fictional portrayals. This cultural fascination with BTK reflects society's broader interest in understanding the minds of serial killers, but it also raises ethical questions about the glorification of criminals and the potential retraumatisation of victims' families.

The BTK case is a stark reminder of the challenges faced by law enforcement in tracking and apprehending serial killers. While advancements in forensic science and policing techniques ultimately led to Rader's capture, his ability to evade detection for decades highlights systemic issues and areas for improvement.

1. The Importance of Interagency Collaboration

One of the key challenges in the BTK case was the lack of communication and coordination between law enforcement agencies. During the 1970s and 1980s, many police departments operated independently, with limited information sharing. This allowed Rader to avoid detection, as investigators in different jurisdictions failed to connect the dots between his crimes.

In the years since Rader's arrest, significant progress has been made in fostering interagency collaboration. Databases like the FBI's Violent Criminal Apprehension Program (ViCAP) allow law enforcement to track and link crimes across jurisdictions, increasing the likelihood of identifying serial offenders.

2. The Role of Forensic Science

Rader's capture was made possible by advancements in forensic science, particularly DNA profiling. In the 1970s and 1980s, DNA evidence was not widely used or understood, leaving investigators with limited tools to link crime scenes to suspects. By 2005, however, DNA technology had become a critical component of criminal investigations. The decision to test DNA from Rader's daughter, Kerri, was a turning point in the case, providing the evidence needed to confirm his identity as BTK.

The BTK case underscores the importance of preserving evidence, even in cold cases. Items collected from crime scenes in the 1970s were crucial in linking Rader to his murders decades later. This highlights the need for meticulous evidence handling and storage, as well as continued investment in forensic technologies.

3. The Danger of Media Involvement

Throughout his killing spree, Rader taunted law enforcement and the media, sending letters, poems, and other communications that revealed details of his crimes. While these communications provided valuable insights into his psychology, they also posed challenges for investigators, as they risked creating public panic and potentially influencing the killer's behaviour.

The media's role in the BTK case is a double-edged sword. On one hand, media coverage kept the case in the public eye, generating tips and maintaining pressure on law enforcement. On the other hand, sensationalist reporting may have emboldened Rader, feeding his narcissism and need for recognition. This raises important questions about how the media should report on serial killers in a way that balances public awareness with ethical responsibility.

Dennis Rader's case has provided criminologists and psychologists with valuable insights into the mind of a serial killer. His ability to live a double life, his methods of control, and his motivations for killing have been extensively studied, offering lessons for understanding and identifying similar offenders.

1. The Narcissistic Killer

Rader's behaviour was driven by a deep-seated need for control, power, and recognition. His taunts to law enforcement and the media reflect his narcissistic tendencies, as he sought to assert his superiority and maintain his status as an elusive predator. He viewed his victims not as individuals but as objects to fulfil his fantasies, showing a complete lack of empathy.

Understanding narcissism in serial killers is crucial for profiling and identifying offenders. Narcissistic killers like Rader often seek attention and validation, which can manifest in behaviours such as taunting, staging crime scenes, or leaving deliberate clues.

2. The Role of Compartmentalisation

One of the most striking aspects of Rader's personality was his ability to compartmentalise his life. He lived as a devoted husband, father, and church leader while secretly carrying out his crimes. This duality allowed him to evade suspicion and maintain his facade of normalcy.

This ability to compartmentalise is a common trait among serial killers, enabling them to blend into society and avoid detection. Understanding this psychological mechanism can help law enforcement identify patterns of behaviour that may indicate hidden deviance.

3. The Development of Fantasies

Rader's crimes were rooted in fantasies of control and domination that began in childhood. His early fascination with bondage, voyeurism, and sadistic imagery evolved into a compulsion to act out these fantasies through murder. This progression underscores the importance of addressing early warning signs of violent behaviour, such as animal cruelty, voyeurism, or obsessive fantasies.

The families of Rader's victims have borne the brunt of his actions, enduring unimaginable grief and trauma. For them, the legacy of BTK is deeply personal, marked by loss, anger, and the long road to healing.

1. The Pain of Losing Loved Ones

Rader's victims were sons, daughters, mothers, and fathers, each with dreams, relationships, and futures stolen by his actions. Their families were left to grapple with the sudden and violent loss of their loved ones, as well as the unanswered questions that lingered for decades before Rader's capture.

2. The Impact of His Reemergence

Rader's decision to resurface in 2004 brought renewed pain for the victims' families. His letters, taunts, and media appearances forced them to relive their losses and confront the reality of his lack of remorse. For many, the trial provided a measure of closure, but the emotional scars remain.

3. Honouring the Victims

In the years since Rader's capture, efforts have been made to honour the victims and preserve their memories. Memorials, advocacy groups, and public awareness campaigns have ensured that the victims are not forgotten, even as the focus on Rader himself diminishes.

The BTK case has left a lasting impact on society, influencing how we approach crime prevention, criminal justice, and public safety.

1. Raising Public Awareness

Rader's ability to live a double life highlights the importance of vigilance in recognising potential red flags. Public awareness campaigns about warning signs of predatory behaviour can help communities identify and report suspicious activities.

2. Improving Criminal Justice Practices

The case underscores the need for continuous improvement in forensic science, law enforcement training, and interagency collaboration. Advances in DNA technology, data sharing, and criminal profiling have already transformed the field, making it harder for offenders like Rader to evade capture.

3. Ethical Considerations in True Crime Media

The cultural fascination with serial killers, exemplified by the attention given to BTK, raises ethical questions about how these cases are portrayed. Balancing the need for public awareness with sensitivity toward victims and their families remains a challenge for the media and entertainment industries.

4
Nannie Doss: "The Giggling Granny"

Nannie Doss, known infamously as "The Giggling Granny," "The Lonely Hearts Killer," and "The Jolly Black Widow," presents one of the most chilling contradictions in the annals of true crime. Behind her cheerful demeanour and infectious laughter lurked a cold-blooded killer who murdered at least 11 people, including husbands, children, grandchildren, and other family members, over a span of three decades. Her nickname, a result of her jovial attitude during police interrogations, belied the gruesome reality of her actions, making her one of the most notorious female serial killers in American history.

Born into poverty in the early 20th century, Nannie's early life was marked by abuse, neglect, and a longing for romance—a desire that ultimately led her down a dark path. Using personal ads in lonely hearts columns to lure her victims, she left a trail of death in her wake, fuelled by greed, resentment, and, as she often claimed, her quest for true love.

What makes Nannie Doss particularly unsettling is her choice of victims: people closest to her, those who trusted her implicitly. She exploited societal expectations of women at the time—caring wives, nurturing mothers, doting grandmothers—to hide her crimes in plain sight. Her modus operandi, often involving poisoning with arsenic-laced meals, allowed her to act undetected for years, while her laughter and charm deflected suspicion.

This chapter delves into the life and crimes of Nannie Doss, tracing her journey from a troubled childhood to a string of murders that shocked the nation. It explores how a woman who seemed the epitome of domesticity turned out to be one of America's most chilling serial killers, and how she ultimately met justice. Behind the facade of the smiling grandmother lay a woman whose pursuit of love and control left destruction in its path—a legacy of laughter masking unthinkable cruelty.

Nannie Doss, born Nancy Hazel on November 4, 1905, in Blue Mountain, Alabama, came into the world under circumstances that would shape her dark and tumultuous future. The story of her early life is one of hardship, deprivation, and unfulfilled dreams, laying the groundwork for the twisted path she would later take. Raised in a strict and abusive household during a time of poverty and limited opportunities for women, Nannie's childhood was marked by emotional neglect, physical hardship, and an escape into fantasy. These formative experiences would eventually manifest in her adult life as manipulation, violence, and a ruthless pursuit of control.

This chapter delves into the conditions and events of Nannie's early life, exploring how they contributed to her psychological development and the eventual transformation into "The Giggling Granny."

Nannie was the first of five children born to James and Louisa Hazel, a poor farming couple struggling to make ends meet in rural Alabama. Life in Blue Mountain was hard; the family worked tirelessly to eke out a living on their small farm. As a child, Nannie was expected to contribute to the household labor, helping with chores, farming duties, and raising her younger siblings. The long hours of backbreaking work left little time for education or leisure, and Nannie's childhood was defined by deprivation and monotony.

James Hazel was a strict and authoritarian figure who ruled his household with an iron fist. He demanded absolute obedience from his children and controlled every aspect of their lives, particularly Nannie's. James's rigid and oppressive parenting style stifled any sense of freedom or individuality in his children, fostering resentment and a longing for escape. This control extended to the children's schooling; James frequently pulled them out of school to work on the farm, leaving Nannie with only a minimal education. Her lack of formal schooling would later limit her opportunities, further fuelling her bitterness and sense of entrapment.

Louisa Hazel, in contrast, was a more passive and nurturing figure, though she often deferred to her husband's authority. Nannie's relationship with her mother was complex. While Louisa provided some measure of affection, she was unable to shield her children from James's overbearing rule. As a result, Nannie grew up feeling both neglected and powerless, a dynamic that would play a significant role in shaping her later need for control.

One pivotal event in Nannie's childhood occurred when she was just seven years old. During a family train journey, the young girl was thrown forward when the train came to an abrupt stop, slamming her head against a metal bar on the seat in front of her. The blow left her unconscious and resulted in chronic headaches, blackouts, and mood swings that would persist throughout her life.

This head injury has been the subject of much speculation among psychologists and criminologists. It is widely believed that traumatic brain injuries, particularly those sustained in childhood, can lead to changes in behaviour and personality. In Nannie's case, the injury may have exacerbated underlying psychological vulnerabilities, contributing to the violent and impulsive tendencies she exhibited later in life. While it is impossible to determine the exact impact of the accident, it marked a turning point in her development and set the stage for the troubling behaviours that would follow.

Amid the harsh realities of her upbringing, Nannie found solace in escapism. From an early age, she developed a fascination with romance magazines, particularly the ones that featured stories of love, passion, and happy endings. These magazines offered her a glimpse into a world far removed from the drudgery of farm life and the oppressive rule of her father. Nannie would later recall spending hours poring over these stories, dreaming of a life filled with romance, excitement, and adoration.

However, this obsession with romance also planted dangerous seeds. The idealised relationships portrayed in the magazines often featured dominant, charismatic men and women who found happiness through submission and devotion. Nannie internalised these narratives, developing unrealistic expectations about love and relationships. She began to equate happiness with finding the "perfect man," someone who could whisk her away from her miserable life and fulfil her fantasies of romantic bliss. This yearning for an idealised love would drive many of her decisions in adulthood, often with deadly consequences.

As Nannie entered adolescence, her resentment toward her father grew. James Hazel's strict rules extended to controlling his daughters' social lives. He forbade them from wearing makeup or fashionable clothing, believing these to be immoral. He also restricted their interactions with boys, refusing to allow them to attend social gatherings or dances. While James likely believed he was protecting his daughters' virtue, his actions only deepened Nannie's sense of isolation and frustration.

These restrictions were particularly painful for Nannie, who yearned for the freedom to explore the romantic ideals she had read about in her magazines. She began to rebel in small ways, sneaking out to attend dances or secretly meeting boys. These acts of defiance provided her with a sense of agency, though they also heightened the tension within the Hazel household.

Nannie's strained relationship with her father also affected her perception of men in general. While she craved love and affection, her experiences with James left her distrustful and resentful of male authority. This ambivalence—longing for connection while resenting control—would define many of her future relationships and contribute to her escalating violence.

While Nannie's father was the dominant force in her childhood, her early experiences also included other forms of abuse that likely influenced her later behaviour. In interviews and confessions, Nannie alluded to being sexually abused by male relatives during her youth. Though she never provided specific details, these experiences left deep emotional scars and may have contributed to her complex feelings about men, power, and control.

Survivors of childhood abuse often struggle with issues of trust, self-worth, and anger, and many develop maladaptive coping mechanisms to deal with their trauma. For Nannie, the combination of abuse, neglect, and a stifling home environment created a volatile mix of emotions that would later manifest in destructive ways.

While much of Nannie's childhood behaviour was typical for a girl living under oppressive conditions, there were early signs that hinted at her darker tendencies. She was described as moody and withdrawn, prone to bouts of anger and defiance. Her fascination with romantic fantasies sometimes took on obsessive qualities, and she displayed a tendency to idealise and then vilify those around her.

Nannie's early exposure to manipulation as a means of survival also became evident. Living in a household dominated by her father's authoritarian rule, she learned to navigate power dynamics by being cunning and deceptive. These traits, while initially a coping mechanism, would later evolve into a means of exerting control over others.

At the age of 16, Nannie found what she believed to be her escape from her father's control: marriage. In 1921, she married Charley Braggs, a co-worker from the linen factory where she had taken a job. Charley, a shy and unassuming young man, seemed to offer Nannie the promise of freedom and the romantic life she had always dreamed of. However, this marriage would prove to be anything but a fairy tale.

Charley's overbearing mother moved in with the couple shortly after their wedding, creating a new dynamic of control and conflict. Nannie quickly found herself trapped once again, this time under the watchful eye of her mother-in-law. The couple's relationship deteriorated as Nannie's resentment grew, and the marriage became marked by infidelity, arguments, and mutual distrust. It was during this period that the first signs of Nannie's capacity for violence began to emerge.

Early Marriages on the Path to Darkness

The early marriages of Nannie Doss, often referred to as "The Giggling Granny," marked the beginning of her descent into a life of manipulation, deceit, and murder. These relationships, shaped by her tumultuous upbringing and unfulfilled desires for romance, laid the foundation for the pattern of violence that would define her life. Each marriage began with promises of love and stability but ended in betrayal, bitterness, and in many cases, death. By examining her early relationships, we can trace how Nannie transitioned from a disillusioned wife seeking escape to a cold-blooded killer driven by greed, control, and resentment.

At the age of 16, Nannie Doss married Charley Braggs, a young man she met while working at a linen factory in her hometown of Blue Mountain, Alabama. For Nannie, this marriage represented her first real opportunity to escape the oppressive control of her father, James Hazel, whose authoritarian rule had dominated her childhood. Charley, a shy and mild-mannered man, seemed to offer Nannie a chance at the romantic life she had always dreamed of.

However, the reality of their marriage was far from Nannie's fantasies. Charley's mother, an overbearing and controlling woman, moved in with the couple shortly after their wedding. Her presence created immediate tension in the household, as she constantly interfered in their relationship and demanded Charley's attention. Nannie, who had spent her entire life under her father's strict rule, found herself trapped in yet another stifling dynamic where her desires and autonomy were overshadowed.

The tension in the Braggs household quickly escalated. Nannie grew resentful of her mother-in-law's influence and Charley's inability to stand up to her. The relationship, initially fuelled by youthful optimism, began to deteriorate as arguments and accusations became commonplace. Nannie's disillusionment with marriage deepened, and she reportedly began drinking heavily to cope with her frustrations.

The couple had four daughters in rapid succession, further straining their already fragile relationship. The stress of raising children in a hostile environment took its toll on Nannie, whose dreams of a romantic and idyllic life seemed more distant than ever. She began to lash out, expressing her anger through manipulation and, eventually, violence.

In 1927, tragedy struck the Braggs household when two of Nannie's daughters died suddenly under suspicious circumstances. The children, both toddlers, were initially believed to have succumbed to food poisoning. However, years later, these deaths would be reevaluated in light of Nannie's later crimes. It is now widely believed that she poisoned the children with arsenic, a substance she would use repeatedly in her future murders.

While the exact motive for these killings remains unclear, they marked a turning point in Nannie's life. The deaths of her children may have been driven by stress, resentment, or even an attempt to punish Charley for his perceived failings as a husband. Whatever the reason, this early act of violence set a chilling precedent for the rest of her life.

By the late 1920s, Charley had grown increasingly suspicious of Nannie's behaviour. He accused her of infidelity, pointing to her frequent disappearances and her habit of reading romance magazines as signs that she was seeking love elsewhere. Fearing for his safety and the safety of their surviving children, Charley took their eldest daughter, Melvina, and fled. He later claimed that he was terrified of Nannie and believed she was capable of harming him.

The couple divorced in 1928, leaving Nannie alone with their youngest daughter, Florine. Charley later described his ex-wife as "the most evil woman I ever met," a statement that foreshadowed the darkness that would define Nannie's future.

Nannie's second marriage, to **Robert Harrelson**, began in 1929, just a year after her divorce from Charley Braggs. The two met through a lonely hearts column, a medium that Nannie would use repeatedly to find future husbands and victims. At first, Robert seemed to embody the romantic ideal that Nannie had always sought. He was charming, attentive, and willing to take on the role of a provider.

However, Robert's true nature soon emerged. He was a heavy drinker and had a violent temper, traits that made their marriage tumultuous from the start. Despite these issues, Nannie stayed with Robert for 16 years—a period marked by escalating dysfunction and abuse.

The relationship between Nannie and Robert was volatile, with frequent arguments and episodes of domestic violence. Robert's drinking exacerbated the tension, as his erratic behaviour often left Nannie feeling humiliated and powerless. To cope, she once again turned to her romance magazines and began fantasising about escape.

Nannie's resentment toward Robert grew over time, and she began to view him as an obstacle to her happiness. This perception, combined with her growing comfort with using violence to solve problems, set the stage for yet another tragedy.

In 1945, Robert Harrelson became Nannie's second known victim. After an argument that escalated into physical violence, Nannie decided to put an end to their troubled marriage—permanently. She laced Robert's corn whiskey with arsenic, a poison she had become familiar with through her reading and research.

Robert's death was initially attributed to alcohol poisoning, as his heavy drinking made this a plausible explanation. Nannie played the role of the grieving widow, concealing her involvement in his death and collecting the small life insurance policy she had taken out on him. This murder marked the beginning of a pattern that Nannie would repeat in her subsequent relationships: using poison to eliminate those who stood in the way of her desires.

After Robert's death, Nannie wasted no time seeking out her next husband. She returned to the lonely hearts columns, where she met Arlie Lanning, a man who seemed to offer stability and companionship. The two married in 1947, and Nannie moved to his home in North Carolina.

Arlie, like Robert, turned out to be an alcoholic with a penchant for infidelity. However, Nannie had learned how to navigate such relationships, using her charm and manipulation to maintain control. She played the role of the devoted wife in public, earning the sympathy and admiration of her neighbours, while quietly plotting Arlie's demise.

In 1952, Arlie died suddenly, his symptoms resembling those of a heart attack. Once again, Nannie had used arsenic to eliminate her husband. As she had done before, she capitalised on the situation by collecting Arlie's life insurance payout. To further deflect suspicion, she feigned grief and ensured that Arlie's death was attributed to natural causes.

Nannie's fourth marriage, to Richard Morton, followed a similar pattern. The two married in 1952, and Nannie moved to Kansas to live with him. Richard, unlike her previous husbands, was not an alcoholic, but he had a wandering eye and often cheated on Nannie with other women.

Nannie's resentment of Richard grew quickly, and she began planning his murder. However, before she could act, she was distracted by another opportunity for violence: the death of her own mother. Nannie invited her elderly mother, Louisa, to live with her and Richard, only to poison her shortly after her arrival. Louisa's death, like the others, was attributed to natural causes.

Richard Morton met his end in 1953, poisoned by Nannie in the same manner as her previous victims. Once again, she played the role of the grieving widow, collecting financial benefits and moving on to her next target.

By the time of her fourth marriage, Nannie Doss had fully embraced her role as a serial killer. Her early experiences with manipulation and violence had evolved into a calculated pattern of behaviour, driven by a combination of greed, resentment, and a twisted sense of justice. She saw her victims—whether husbands, family members, or children—as obstacles to her happiness, disposable pawns in her quest for control and financial security.

Nannie's ability to blend into her surroundings and play the role of a loving wife or grieving widow allowed her to operate undetected for decades. Her use of arsenic, a poison that mimicked the symptoms of natural illnesses, further obscured her crimes. By the time law enforcement began to suspect foul play, Nannie had already claimed multiple lives and left a trail of devastation in her wake.

The Lonely Hearts Killer: A Pattern Emerges

By the mid-20th century, Nannie Doss had begun to master a horrifying method of seeking out victims under the guise of love and companionship. Through the use of lonely hearts columns, a popular avenue for personal ads at the time, she systematically identified men who were emotionally vulnerable or in search of a partner, luring them into relationships that would eventually end in death. Her charm, wit, and seemingly warm personality masked her dark intentions, allowing her to move from one victim to the next with chilling efficiency.

This chapter delves into the evolution of Nannie's calculated approach as "The Lonely Hearts Killer," uncovering how she exploited societal norms, manipulated her victims, and honed a pattern of violence that left authorities baffled for years. While her earlier marriages were marred by dysfunction, it was through lonely hearts ads that Nannie perfected her deadly routine, creating a path littered with heartbreak, betrayal, and murder.

Lonely hearts columns became a lifeline for people seeking romance, companionship, or a second chance at love during the 1940s and 1950s. For women like Nannie, who knew how to manipulate appearances, these columns were an ideal hunting ground. Nannie's ads and responses were carefully crafted to appeal to the needs and vulnerabilities of potential suitors. She presented herself as a sweet, caring, and devoted woman—someone who would offer stability, affection, and loyalty.

This facade was particularly effective in post-Depression and post-War America, where widowers and single men often sought women who could provide comfort and companionship in their later years. Lonely hearts ads operated on a foundation of trust, as people were often willing to overlook red flags in the hopes of finding genuine connection. Nannie's cheerful and disarming demeanour allowed her to build that trust quickly.

Nannie's approach to her victims was methodical. Once she identified a suitable match through the lonely hearts columns, she would correspond with her targets through letters, charming them with promises of devotion and shared happiness. Often, these men were seeking a caregiver or someone to bring warmth into their lives, making them easy prey for Nannie's manipulative tactics.

Once a relationship was established, Nannie worked quickly to secure her position in her victim's life, often moving into their homes or encouraging rapid marriages. Her ability to ingratiate herself with her victims' families and communities made her seem trustworthy and reliable. This swift integration allowed her to plan her crimes with minimal suspicion.

A clear pattern emerged as Nannie moved through her lonely hearts victims. Her approach to eliminating her husbands and other victims followed a consistent method, rooted in her preferred use of arsenic. This poison was both accessible and difficult to detect at the time, allowing Nannie to carry out her murders without drawing significant attention.

1. **Stalking Emotional Vulnerabilities:**

Nannie often targeted men who had experienced personal loss or were socially isolated. These men were more likely to overlook warning signs or inconsistencies in her behaviour, making them ideal victims.

2. **Building Trust Quickly:**

By presenting herself as a nurturing and loving partner, Nannie quickly gained the trust of her victims and their families. Her charm and good humour disarmed suspicion, even as she began to manipulate those around her.

3. **Manipulating Financials:**
Financial gain was a significant motivator in many of Nannie's murders. She often ensured that life insurance policies were taken out in her name, or she positioned herself to inherit money and property. Her victims' deaths were frequently timed to coincide with the activation of these policies, ensuring maximum profit.

4. **Administering Poison:**
Arsenic became Nannie's weapon of choice. She laced her victims' food or drinks, often cooking meals that appeared to be expressions of love and care. The poison worked gradually, mimicking symptoms of natural illnesses like food poisoning or heart failure, making her crimes difficult to detect.

5. **Feigning Grief:**
After her victims' deaths, Nannie portrayed herself as a grieving widow, ensuring that suspicions were directed elsewhere. Her ability to maintain a cheerful facade, even while feigning grief, earned her the chilling nickname, "The Giggling Granny."

Victims of the Lonely Hearts Killer

Frank Harrelson

Nannie met Frank Harrelson through a lonely hearts column in the 1940s. At first, their relationship appeared to bring stability to Nannie's life. However, Frank's heavy drinking and violent temper soon turned their marriage toxic. When Frank's behaviour became unbearable, Nannie resorted to her signature solution: arsenic. His death was attributed to heart failure, allowing Nannie to escape suspicion and move on to her next victim.

Arlie Lanning

Arlie Lanning, another lonely hearts victim, became Nannie's third husband. Arlie's death followed a similar pattern—initial happiness, escalating tension, and a sudden, unexplained illness. After his death, Nannie used her charm to deflect attention, convincing the community that she was a devoted wife who had done everything to care for her ailing husband.

Richard Morton

Nannie's fourth husband, Richard Morton, fell victim not long after their marriage. While Richard's infidelity strained their relationship, it was Nannie's greed that sealed his fate. Like her previous victims, Richard was poisoned with arsenic, and his death allowed Nannie to collect yet another life insurance payout.

Part of Nannie's success as a serial killer lay in her ability to exploit societal expectations of women at the time. In mid-20th century America, women were often viewed as nurturers and caregivers, roles that Nannie played to perfection. Her cheerful disposition and grandmotherly appearance made her seem incapable of violence, allowing her to operate undetected for decades.

Additionally, societal norms often placed women in positions of financial dependence on their husbands. Nannie turned this dynamic on its head, using her marriages as a means of financial gain and eliminating her husbands when they were no longer useful. Her actions were a subversion of traditional gender roles, using them as a shield while committing acts of betrayal and murder.

As "The Lonely Hearts Killer," Nannie Doss exhibited traits consistent with psychopathy and narcissism. Her ability to manipulate and deceive others, combined with her lack of empathy, allowed her to rationalise her crimes and maintain her cheerful facade. Nannie's murders were not crimes of passion but calculated acts driven by greed, resentment, and a twisted sense of entitlement.

Her obsession with romance and the pursuit of the "perfect love" also played a significant role in her behaviour. When her relationships inevitably failed to meet her unrealistic expectations, Nannie responded with violence, seeing murder as a means of regaining control.

One of the most remarkable aspects of Nannie's killing spree was her ability to evade detection for so long. Several factors contributed to her success:

- **Medical Limitations:**

At the time, arsenic poisoning was difficult to detect without a thorough autopsy, and many of Nannie's victims were believed to have died of natural causes.

- **Societal Perception:**

Nannie's gender and cheerful demeanour made her an unlikely suspect in the eyes of law enforcement and the public. She used these perceptions to her advantage, deflecting suspicion and shifting blame.

- **Geographic Mobility:**

By frequently relocating and marrying men in different states, Nannie avoided drawing attention to the pattern of deaths that followed her.

Despite her cunning and adaptability, Nannie's pattern eventually began to unravel. Her overconfidence and repeated use of arsenic raised suspicions, particularly after the death of her fifth husband, Samuel Doss, in 1954. Samuel's death prompted a thorough investigation, including an autopsy that revealed lethal levels of arsenic in his system. This discovery set in motion the events that would lead to Nannie's arrest and the end of her deadly reign.

Family Ties and Betrayal: Killing Those Closest

Nannie Doss, celebrated for her cheerful demeanour but infamous for her heinous crimes, shattered the sanctity of familial trust in ways that remain deeply unsettling. While her husbands' deaths were often linked to greed or dissatisfaction, her decision to turn on her own family members revealed a far darker pattern. Unlike her spouses, whose relationships were often brief and transactional, her family represented deeper, lifelong connections, yet they became some of her most tragic victims. This chapter explores how Nannie's betrayals within her family exposed her complete disregard for human life, her ability to manipulate familial bonds, and the true depths of her depravity.

Nannie Doss's children were among her earliest victims of betrayal. As a mother, she was expected to nurture and protect, but her actions contradicted these fundamental principles of motherhood. The first signs of Nannie's capacity for violence against her family surfaced during her marriage to Charley Braggs, her first husband.

Nannie and Charley had four daughters during their tumultuous marriage. In 1927, tragedy struck the family when two of their daughters, both toddlers, died suddenly. The deaths were attributed to suspected food poisoning at the time, but in light of Nannie's later confessions and patterns, it is now believed that she poisoned the children with arsenic. The true motive behind their deaths remains unclear—whether driven by frustration, the stress of raising multiple children, or a twisted attempt to punish Charley during their deteriorating marriage. These deaths marked the first known instance of Nannie using poison to solve her personal problems, establishing a pattern that would persist for decades.

Two of Nannie's daughters, Melvina and Florine, survived their mother's deadly spree, though their lives were far from free of trauma. Growing up in a household fraught with dysfunction and tragedy, they were deeply affected by the loss of their siblings. Melvina, in particular, maintained a complicated relationship with her mother, marked by love, suspicion, and betrayal.

Years after Nannie's initial crimes, her violence resurfaced in the most unthinkable way: the murder of her own grandchild. Following her daughter Melvina's marriage and the birth of Melvina's children, Nannie remained actively involved in their lives. Her cheerful and doting persona gave no hint of her true intentions.

In 1945, Melvina gave birth to a healthy baby boy. Shortly after the delivery, Nannie visited her daughter in the hospital to offer support. However, the visit took a sinister turn when the newborn died under suspicious circumstances. Melvina later claimed that she had seen her mother holding a hatpin near the baby's head shortly before his death, raising suspicions that Nannie had intentionally killed the child.

Although Melvina voiced her concerns to other family members, no formal investigation took place. In the aftermath, the baby's death was attributed to unknown causes, allowing Nannie to escape scrutiny. This incident underscores her willingness to exploit moments of vulnerability, even at the expense of her own family.

Not content with taking one life, Nannie's lethal tendencies extended to another of Melvina's children, Robert Lee. At just two years old, Robert died suddenly while in Nannie's care. His death, like so many others, was attributed to food poisoning, but the circumstances and Nannie's history suggest arsenic poisoning. This loss devastated Melvina, further straining her relationship with her mother and creating an enduring legacy of grief and suspicion.

Among Nannie's most shocking betrayals was her decision to murder her own mother, **Louisa Hazel**. After a lifetime of complicated relationships, Nannie invited her elderly mother to live with her following the death of her fourth husband, Richard Morton. Louisa, unaware of her daughter's dark past, accepted the invitation, likely seeing it as an opportunity for support in her later years.

Shortly after moving into Nannie's home, Louisa fell gravely ill. Within a short period, she died, with her symptoms eerily consistent with arsenic poisoning. As with many of Nannie's crimes, Louisa's death was not immediately questioned. Nannie played the role of the grieving daughter, ensuring that no suspicion fell on her. Her ability to murder her own mother demonstrated her complete lack of moral boundaries and underscored her readiness to eliminate anyone she saw as an inconvenience or obstacle.

Nannie's pattern of betrayal extended beyond her immediate family to include siblings, grandchildren, and other relatives. Each of these murders followed a chillingly consistent pattern of manipulation, exploitation, and calculated violence.

One of Nannie's lesser-known crimes involved her sister, **Dovie Hazel**, who was suffering from a chronic illness. Nannie invited Dovie to stay with her under the guise of offering care and support, but instead, she saw Dovie's presence as a burden. It wasn't long before Dovie died suddenly, and while her death was attributed to natural causes, the timing and circumstances strongly suggest that Nannie poisoned her.

While many of Nannie's murders were fuelled by personal grievances or convenience, financial gain also played a significant role. She often ensured that life insurance policies were taken out on her family members, positioning herself as the beneficiary. This financial incentive drove her to eliminate relatives who posed no direct threat but whose deaths would result in monetary rewards.

Nannie was known to encourage or insist on life insurance policies for her victims, citing practical reasons like financial security for the family. However, these policies invariably became tools of murder.

After collecting payouts following the deaths of her husbands, children, and grandchildren, Nannie built a pattern that combined personal gain with her deadly methods.

Nannie's actions left a profound and lasting impact on her family. The loss of so many loved ones, combined with the revelation of her crimes, created a legacy of trauma that haunted surviving relatives. Those who lived through her betrayals faced not only the grief of losing family members but also the horror of discovering that the person responsible was someone they had trusted implicitly.

Melvina, who lost both a newborn and a toddler to her mother's actions, carried the emotional scars of Nannie's betrayal for the rest of her life. The sense of betrayal and the unanswered questions surrounding her children's deaths were compounded by the knowledge that her mother had so deliberately and coldly orchestrated their demise.

One of the most disturbing aspects of Nannie's familial crimes was her ability to manipulate trust and power dynamics. Family relationships are inherently built on trust, making her betrayal all the more shocking. Nannie used societal expectations of women—especially mothers and grandmothers—as caregivers and nurturers to her advantage, disarming suspicion and ensuring that her victims felt safe in her presence.

Nannie's cheerful demeanour and maternal role made her an unlikely suspect in the eyes of law enforcement and her community. By playing into the stereotype of the doting grandmother or selfless caregiver, she masked her true intentions and avoided detection for years.

Ultimately, Nannie Doss's decision to target her family members revealed the full extent of her ruthlessness. Unlike her husbands, who were often strangers when she met them, her family represented deep, lifelong bonds. Yet she viewed these relationships not as sacred but as opportunities for exploitation. Her willingness to kill those closest to her underscores her lack of empathy, her obsession with control, and her belief that human life was expendable.

The Downfall: Samuel Doss and the End of a Killing Spree

By the early 1950s, Nannie Doss, also known as "The Giggling Granny," had perfected her method of killing, leaving a string of dead husbands, children, grandchildren, and other family members in her wake. Her life of deception and murder spanned decades, with no one suspecting that the cheerful grandmother with a love for romance novels was a serial killer. However, her final victim, Samuel Doss, unwittingly became the key to her downfall. His death, unlike her previous murders, triggered an investigation that unraveled her web of lies and ultimately exposed her horrifying crimes.

This chapter explores the life and death of Samuel Doss, how his murder led to the discovery of Nannie's heinous acts, and the critical mistakes she made that ended her killing spree.

Samuel Doss entered Nannie's life in 1953, shortly after the death of her fourth husband, Richard Morton. Samuel, a widower living in Tulsa, Oklahoma, was a stark contrast to Nannie's previous victims. He was a conservative, devoutly religious man who valued structure and discipline, traits that likely appealed to Nannie as she sought her next target. The couple met through a lonely hearts column, a medium Nannie had used repeatedly to find her victims. Samuel, lonely after the death of his first wife and eager for companionship, fell for Nannie's charm and promises of a loving partnership.

Their relationship progressed quickly, and the couple married soon after meeting. To Samuel, Nannie appeared to be the ideal wife—cheerful, attentive, and eager to build a life together. However, as with her previous marriages, Nannie's intentions were far from genuine. She likely saw Samuel as another source of financial gain, as he had savings and property that could be exploited.

Unlike many of Nannie's previous husbands, Samuel Doss was neither an alcoholic nor a philanderer. He was a straightforward man who lived a modest life and had no apparent vices. His conservative and disciplined nature, however, clashed with Nannie's personality. Samuel was strict about finances, discouraging frivolous spending and insisting on a practical lifestyle. He even limited Nannie's access to romance magazines, which had long been her source of escapism and inspiration.

For Nannie, these restrictions represented a loss of control, something she could not tolerate. Samuel's frugality and structured approach to life became an irritant, and their marriage quickly began to sour. It was during this time that Nannie started to plan her next move, one that would end Samuel's life and secure her financial independence.

In September 1954, Nannie made her first attempt to kill Samuel. She laced one of his meals with arsenic, her preferred method of murder. Samuel soon fell gravely ill, experiencing severe gastrointestinal distress, fever, and fatigue. However, unlike her previous victims, Samuel survived this initial attempt on his life. Concerned for his health, he sought medical attention and was admitted to a hospital, where he remained for several weeks.

During his hospital stay, Samuel's doctors treated him for what they believed to be a severe digestive illness. Despite his symptoms, no one suspected foul play, and Nannie continued to present herself as a caring and devoted wife. She visited Samuel regularly, offering support and ensuring that no one questioned her role in his illness.

After being discharged from the hospital, Samuel returned home to recuperate. Doctors warned him to rest and follow a strict diet, advice he took seriously. However, his decision to trust Nannie once again would prove fatal.

Shortly after his return, Nannie prepared a meal for Samuel, once again lacing it with arsenic. This time, the dose was lethal. Samuel died on **October 12, 1954**, just days after leaving the hospital. His death was sudden, and his symptoms mirrored those of a heart attack, a diagnosis that would have likely gone unquestioned had it not been for one critical decision.

Unlike Nannie's previous victims, Samuel's death raised suspicions, primarily due to the timing. His recent hospitalisation and unexplained illness before his death prompted his physician to order an autopsy—a routine that had not been performed on Nannie's earlier victims. The autopsy revealed an alarming amount of arsenic in Samuel's system, confirming that he had been poisoned.

This discovery set off a chain reaction that would ultimately lead to Nannie's arrest. The findings from the autopsy were reported to authorities, who began investigating Samuel's death more closely. As investigators dug deeper into Nannie's past, they uncovered a disturbing pattern of sudden and unexplained deaths among her previous husbands and family members.

On **November 26, 1954**, Nannie Doss was arrested in Tulsa, Oklahoma, on suspicion of murder. Initially, she denied any involvement in Samuel's death, maintaining her cheerful demeanour and insisting that she was innocent. However, as evidence mounted against her, Nannie's facade began to crack. Faced with the results of the autopsy and questions about her history, she eventually confessed—not only to killing Samuel but also to the murders of several of her previous husbands and family members.

Nannie's confession was both shocking and revealing. Over the course of several interrogations, she admitted to poisoning four of her husbands, two of her children, her mother, her sister, her grandson, and her mother-in-law. She described her methods in chilling detail, explaining how she used arsenic to lace her victims' food and drinks. Her tone during these confessions was unnervingly cheerful, earning her the nickname "The Giggling Granny." She showed no remorse for her actions, often joking about her crimes and deflecting blame onto her victims.

Nannie's motives varied from case to case but were largely rooted in financial gain, resentment, and a desire for control. She frequently collected life insurance payouts after her victims' deaths, using the money to fund her lifestyle and move on to her next target. In other cases, she killed out of frustration or as a means of escaping relationships that no longer suited her.

Following her confession, authorities exhumed the bodies of several of Nannie's victims to confirm her claims. Autopsies revealed high levels of arsenic in each case, corroborating her accounts and solidifying the case against her. The investigation also uncovered a pattern of suspicious deaths that had gone unnoticed for years, highlighting the gaps in forensic science and law enforcement practices at the time.

Nannie Doss was charged with multiple counts of murder, but prosecutors initially focused on the death of Samuel Doss, as it provided the most concrete evidence. In May 1955, Nannie pleaded guilty to his murder, sparing the state the expense and emotional toll of a lengthy trial.

During sentencing, the court considered the magnitude of her crimes and the danger she posed to society. Nannie was ultimately sentenced to life in prison, a decision influenced by her gender and the era's reluctance to impose the death penalty on women.

The arrest and conviction of Nannie Doss marked the end of her killing spree, but the impact of her crimes reverberated long after her imprisonment. Her case exposed significant shortcomings in how authorities handled suspicious deaths, particularly those involving poison. It also raised questions about the societal norms that allowed her to operate undetected for so long.

Nannie's cheerful demeanour and shocking confessions captivated the public, making her one of the most infamous female serial killers in history. Her story has been the subject of books, documentaries, and true crime discussions, serving as a grim reminder of how easily trust can be exploited.

The Giggling Confession

When Nannie Doss was finally apprehended in November 1954, her confession became one of the most bizarre and chilling aspects of her criminal story. Dubbed "The Giggling Granny" due to her unsettling demeanour, Nannie recounted her crimes with a shocking lack of remorse, frequently laughing and joking as she detailed how she had poisoned family members, friends, and husbands alike. Her confession painted a picture of a woman who saw murder as a practical solution to her problems, driven by greed, resentment, and, in some cases, sheer convenience.

This chapter delves into the unique circumstances of Nannie Doss's confession, the disturbing mindset it revealed, and its lasting impact on both law enforcement and society's understanding of female serial killers.

Following the death of her fifth husband, Samuel Doss, suspicions about Nannie's involvement began to grow. The discovery of arsenic in Samuel's body during an autopsy prompted police to investigate Nannie's past, uncovering a pattern of suspicious deaths linked to her. By the time she was brought in for questioning, investigators were already piecing together the puzzle of her crimes.

Despite the mounting evidence against her, Nannie remained calm, even cheerful. From the outset of her interrogation, she displayed none of the panic or defensiveness typically associated with accused murderers. Instead, she seemed eager to talk, as though the weight of her secrets had finally become too much to bear.

When investigators confronted Nannie with the evidence against her, she offered little resistance. Unlike many criminals who deny their involvement or attempt to deflect blame, Nannie admitted to her crimes with astonishing ease. She even seemed pleased to share the details, as if recounting amusing anecdotes from her life.

One of the most unsettling aspects of her confession was her demeanour. Nannie laughed and smiled throughout the interrogation, often cracking jokes or making light of the horrors she described. Her giggling, which earned her the infamous nickname "The Giggling Granny," baffled investigators. It was clear that Nannie did not view her actions with the gravity they deserved; instead, she appeared to find them amusing, perhaps even entertaining.

Over the course of her confession, Nannie admitted to murdering four of her husbands, two of her children, her mother, her sister, her grandson, and her mother-in-law. The sheer scale of her crimes was staggering, but what shocked investigators even more was the casual manner in which she discussed them.

The Motives

While Nannie's motives varied slightly from case to case, they often boiled down to three main factors:

1. **Financial Gain:**

Nannie frequently cited life insurance policies as a driving force behind her murders. She ensured that her victims had policies in place, with herself as the beneficiary, before orchestrating their deaths.

2. **Control and Convenience:**

Many of Nannie's victims were killed simply because they had become inconvenient to her. Whether it was a husband who didn't meet her romantic expectations or a family member who required care, Nannie saw murder as a practical way to regain control of her life.

3. **Emotional Resentment:**

In some cases, Nannie acted out of spite or frustration. Her cheerful demeanour masked deep-seated anger and resentment, which she expressed through her lethal actions.

Nannie's preferred method of murder was arsenic poisoning, which she described in detail during her confession. She often laced her victims' food or drinks with the poison, choosing meals that would seem like acts of love and care—pies, coffee, and stews. The choice of arsenic was calculated; it was accessible, effective, and difficult to detect at the time.

Perhaps the most chilling aspect of Nannie's confession was her complete lack of remorse. She spoke about her victims as though they were obstacles to be removed, not human beings with lives and families. Her giggling and jokes suggested that she viewed her actions as justified or inconsequential, an attitude that horrified those who heard her confession.

Nannie's laughter and jokes may have served as a coping mechanism, a way to deflect from the seriousness of her actions. By treating her crimes as humorous anecdotes, she distanced herself from the reality of what she had done. This behaviour also had the effect of disarming those around her, making it difficult to reconcile the cheerful grandmother with the cold-blooded killer she truly was.

Nannie's lack of empathy and her ability to rationalise her crimes suggest traits commonly associated with sociopathy. She appeared to view her victims as means to an end, rather than as individuals with their own needs and emotions. This mindset allowed her to commit her crimes without guilt or hesitation.

The investigators who interviewed Nannie Doss were deeply affected by her confession. Many had never encountered a killer so candid, cheerful, and unapologetic. Her willingness to discuss her crimes in detail, combined with her unsettling demeanour, left a lasting impression on those who worked on the case.

For many law enforcement officials, it was difficult to believe that a woman who looked and acted like Nannie could be capable of such atrocities. Her grandmotherly appearance and cheerful personality contradicted the stereotype of a serial killer, making her confession all the more shocking.

As Nannie spoke, investigators began to realise the full extent of her crimes. Her confession prompted them to revisit the deaths of her previous husbands and family members, leading to exhumations and further investigations. In case after case, autopsies confirmed her use of arsenic, corroborating her claims and solidifying the case against her.

News of Nannie Doss's confession quickly spread, capturing the attention of the public and the media. Her nickname, "The Giggling Granny," became a symbol of the case, highlighting the macabre juxtaposition between her cheerful demeanour and the heinous nature of her crimes.

Nannie's confession made headlines across the country, with newspapers and radio programs reporting on her bizarre behaviour and shocking admissions. Her story became a topic of fascination, both for the scale of her crimes and the unsettling personality behind them.

The public's reaction to Nannie's confession also highlighted the way her case challenged societal stereotypes about women. At a time when women were often seen as nurturing and harmless, Nannie's actions and attitude forced people to confront the reality that women could also commit calculated and violent crimes.

Nannie's confession provided a rare glimpse into the mind of a female serial killer, offering valuable insights for psychologists and criminologists. Her behaviour and motives have been studied extensively, shedding light on the factors that drove her actions and the traits that allowed her to evade suspicion for so long.

Nannie's ability to rationalise her actions was a key factor in her crimes. She often framed her murders as practical solutions to her problems, whether financial, emotional, or logistical. Over time, this mindset allowed her to escalate her behaviour, moving from one victim to the next with increasing confidence.

Nannie's success as a killer was also rooted in her ability to manipulate those around her. She used her charm and cheerful personality to build trust, ensuring that no one suspected her true intentions. This skill, combined with societal expectations of women, allowed her to operate undetected for decades.

The legacy of Nannie Doss's confession extends beyond the specifics of her case. Her story has had a lasting impact on criminal psychology, forensic science, and public perceptions of female criminals.

Nannie's use of arsenic highlighted the need for advancements in forensic toxicology. Her confession and the subsequent investigations underscored the importance of autopsies and thorough examinations in uncovering cases of poisoning.

Nannie's case has contributed to a deeper understanding of female serial killers, challenging assumptions about their motives, methods, and psychological profiles. Her confession remains a key example of how gendered stereotypes can obscure the true nature of a criminal.

Public Awareness

The widespread coverage of Nannie's confession brought attention to the dangers of unchecked trust and the importance of vigilance, even within familial relationships. Her story serves as a cautionary tale, reminding society that appearances can be deceiving.

The trial and sentencing of Nannie Doss, widely known as "The Giggling Granny," marked the final chapter of one of the most chilling crime sprees in American history. After decades of operating as a serial killer who preyed on her own family and husbands, Nannie's eventual confession in 1954 forced her to face the judicial system. Though the extent of her crimes stretched beyond what the courts could fully address, her trial was pivotal in bringing a measure of justice to her victims and highlighting the cracks in the legal and forensic practices of the time. This chapter examines the legal proceedings that followed Nannie's confession, the challenges faced by prosecutors, and the societal implications of her sentencing.

When Nannie Doss confessed to the murder of multiple husbands and family members, the sheer scope of her crimes presented a logistical challenge for prosecutors. She had admitted to at least 11 murders, spanning multiple states and jurisdictions. Each case would require its own investigation, and trying Nannie for all her crimes would have been both time-consuming and expensive.

Ultimately, prosecutors chose to focus on the death of her fifth husband, **Samuel Doss**, whose autopsy had revealed lethal levels of arsenic. Samuel's murder offered the clearest evidence and the strongest case against her. The autopsy results, coupled with Nannie's detailed confession, made it virtually impossible for her defence team to argue her innocence. Moreover, because Samuel's murder occurred in Oklahoma, a state with clear and enforceable homicide statutes, it became the ideal jurisdiction for the trial.

By centring the trial on Samuel's death, the state avoided the complexities of extradition or coordinating with other states to pursue charges for her additional murders. This pragmatic approach ensured that Nannie would face justice while sparing the victims' families the emotional toll of reliving each crime in court.

From the moment Nannie Doss's crimes became public knowledge, the case captured the nation's attention. Her cheerful demeanour, macabre giggling during her confession, and shocking ability to evade detection for decades fascinated and horrified the public in equal measure. By the time her trial began, Nannie had become a media sensation, with journalists flocking to cover every detail.

Nannie's case defied societal expectations of women, particularly in mid-20th century America. Women were generally viewed as nurturing and incapable of extreme violence, making Nannie's actions all the more shocking. Her crimes challenged deeply ingrained stereotypes and forced the public to grapple with the unsettling reality that women, too, could be calculating and cold-blooded killers.

Her status as an older woman—a grandmother, no less—added another layer of complexity to public perception. Many found it difficult to reconcile her warm, grandmotherly appearance with the horrific nature of her crimes. This disconnect only heightened the fascination surrounding her trial, as people sought to understand how someone so seemingly ordinary could commit such extraordinary acts of violence.

The Prosecution's Case

The prosecution's primary objective was to secure a conviction for Samuel Doss's murder. With Nannie's confession and the autopsy results as their central pieces of evidence, the state presented a straightforward case. Prosecutors detailed how Nannie had poisoned Samuel by lacing his food with arsenic, drawing on testimony from medical experts who confirmed the presence of the poison in his system.

To strengthen their case, prosecutors also introduced evidence of Nannie's pattern of behaviour. While the trial officially focused on Samuel's death, the prosecution highlighted her history of suspicious deaths among her husbands and family members. This pattern demonstrated that Samuel's murder was not an isolated incident but part of a broader series of premeditated killings.

The Defence's Approach

Nannie's defence team faced an uphill battle. The overwhelming evidence against her, combined with her own confession, left little room for a traditional defence strategy. Instead, her attorneys sought to mitigate the consequences of her actions by focusing on her mental state.

The defence argued that Nannie was not of sound mind when she committed her crimes, pointing to her cheerful demeanour during her confession as evidence of psychological instability. They suggested that her actions stemmed from deep-seated emotional trauma and a possible personality disorder, arguing that these factors diminished her culpability.

Despite these arguments, the defence did not pursue an insanity plea, as Nannie had been deemed competent to stand trial. Instead, they aimed to evoke sympathy from the jury, framing her as a deeply troubled woman rather than a cold-blooded killer.

Nannie's trial began in **May 1955** in Tulsa, Oklahoma. While the proceedings were relatively brief, they offered a disturbing glimpse into her mindset and the extent of her crimes.

One of the most anticipated moments of the trial was Nannie's testimony. Her willingness to discuss her crimes in detail, paired with her unnerving giggling, left a lasting impression on everyone present. She recounted how she had poisoned Samuel by adding arsenic to his food, describing the process with a chilling lack of emotion. Her casual demeanour and light-hearted remarks shocked the courtroom, further solidifying her reputation as "The Giggling Granny."

When asked about her motives, Nannie offered vague and contradictory explanations. At times, she framed her actions as acts of self-preservation, claiming that her victims had mistreated or disappointed her. In other moments, she hinted at financial motivations, admitting that life insurance payouts had influenced her decisions. Throughout her testimony, she showed no remorse for her actions, instead treating the proceedings as a bizarre form of entertainment.

The trial also featured testimony from medical experts who detailed the effects of arsenic poisoning. These experts explained how the poison caused a slow and painful death, describing symptoms such as severe abdominal pain, vomiting, and organ failure. Their accounts highlighted the cruelty of Nannie's crimes, underscoring the suffering she had inflicted on her victims.

The jury deliberated for only a short time before delivering their verdict: **guilty of first-degree murder**. The evidence against Nannie was overwhelming, and her lack of remorse left little doubt about her culpability. While Oklahoma law allowed for the death penalty in cases of first-degree murder, the jury opted for a sentence of **life imprisonment without the possibility of parole**.

Several factors influenced the decision to impose a life sentence rather than the death penalty. One key consideration was Nannie's gender. In the 1950s, societal attitudes often framed women as less culpable than men, even in cases of violent crime. The idea of executing an older woman—a grandmother—may have been too unsettling for the jury and the public.

Additionally, Nannie's age likely played a role. At the time of her trial, she was in her late 40s, and a life sentence was seen as a sufficient punishment that would ensure she spent the remainder of her days behind bars.

Following her sentencing, Nannie was transferred to the Oklahoma State Penitentiary, where she spent the remainder of her life. Her time in prison was marked by the same cheerful demeanour she had displayed during her trial. She reportedly enjoyed the attention she received from fellow inmates and prison staff, often joking about her crimes and embracing her notoriety.

Nannie's ability to adapt to her new environment reflected her remarkable resilience and lack of remorse. She quickly became a fixture in the prison community, maintaining her persona as the cheerful grandmother despite the gravity of her crimes. Her continued giggling and lighthearted attitude baffled those around her, serving as a grim reminder of the mindset that had enabled her killing spree.

While Nannie appeared to adjust well to life in prison, her incarceration marked the end of her reign of terror. Stripped of the ability to manipulate and exploit those around her, she was forced to confront the consequences of her actions, even if she showed no outward signs of regret.

The trial and sentencing of Nannie Doss provided a measure of justice for her victims and their families. While the full scope of her crimes could never be fully addressed in a courtroom, her conviction ensured that she would never harm another person. For the families of her victims, the verdict offered some closure, though the pain of their losses would linger for years to come.

Nannie's case became a landmark in the history of criminal justice, highlighting the importance of thorough investigations and the need for advancements in forensic science. Her ability to evade detection for so long exposed significant gaps in how authorities handled suspicious deaths, particularly those involving poison.

Nannie Doss died of leukaemia on **June 2, 1965**, while serving her life sentence. Her death marked the end of one of the most infamous crime sprees in American history, but her legacy as "The Giggling Granny" continues to captivate true crime enthusiasts and criminologists alike.

Legacy of a Killer: Lessons from Nannie Doss

The story of Nannie Doss, infamously known as "The Giggling Granny," serves as a cautionary tale of manipulation, exploitation, and the ability to commit unspeakable acts under the guise of normalcy. Her life and crimes highlight significant societal, legal, and psychological issues, offering lessons that remain relevant today. While her actions shocked mid-20th century America, the broader implications of her case continue to resonate, revealing critical insights into human behaviour, criminal justice, and the vulnerabilities of societal trust.

This chapter explores the enduring legacy of Nannie Doss, focusing on the lessons learned from her actions and their impact on the fields of law enforcement, criminology, and public awareness.

Nannie Doss's ability to blend into society while carrying out her crimes exemplifies the danger of relying on superficial judgments. Her grandmotherly appearance, cheerful demeanour, and seemingly nurturing personality allowed her to evade suspicion for decades. Neighbours, family members, and even law enforcement officers were disarmed by her charm and refused to believe that such a figure could be responsible for cold-blooded murders.

At the time of her crimes, societal norms dictated that women were inherently nurturing and incapable of extreme violence. This stereotype worked to Nannie's advantage, enabling her to avoid scrutiny even as deaths mounted around her. Her case underscores the need to challenge gender-based assumptions in criminal investigations, as such biases can obscure the truth and hinder justice.

Nannie's crimes also serve as a reminder of the importance of vigilance and critical thinking. Her ability to manipulate those around her was rooted in the trust people placed in her based on her outward appearance. While trust is a cornerstone of society, blind trust can create opportunities for exploitation, as demonstrated by Nannie's actions.

Nannie Doss's use of arsenic as her weapon of choice highlighted the limitations of forensic science during her era. At the time, arsenic poisoning was difficult to detect without thorough autopsies, and symptoms often mimicked natural illnesses such as food poisoning or heart failure. This allowed Nannie to carry out her crimes undetected for years, as her victims' deaths were frequently attributed to natural causes.

The Doss case underscored the need for advancements in toxicology and post-mortem examinations. Modern forensic science has made significant strides in detecting poisons and other substances in the human body, making it far more difficult for killers like Nannie to operate undetected. Her case serves as a reminder of the importance of continuous investment in forensic technologies to stay ahead of those who would exploit scientific blind spots.

Another lesson from Nannie's case is the importance of preserving evidence, even in cases initially deemed to be natural deaths. The exhumation of several of her victims' bodies provided crucial evidence that confirmed her confessions, highlighting the value of retaining samples and records for future investigations.

Nannie Doss's case challenged traditional views of serial killers, particularly those related to gender. At the time, most known serial killers were men, and female offenders were rarely studied or understood. Nannie's crimes provided a valuable case study for criminologists, offering insights into the unique characteristics and motivations of female serial killers.

Unlike many male serial killers, who often target strangers or act out of sadistic desires, Nannie's crimes were deeply personal. Her victims were almost exclusively family members or romantic partners, and her motivations often stemmed from financial gain, resentment, or the desire to escape undesirable situations. This pattern aligns with broader trends observed among female serial killers, who are more likely to kill within their immediate social circles.

Nannie's use of arsenic reflects another common trait among female killers: the preference for poison as a weapon. Poison allows for a degree of distance and anonymity, making it an ideal method for those who wish to avoid direct confrontation or physical violence. Understanding these behavioural patterns has helped criminologists develop more nuanced profiles of female offenders, improving the ability to identify and apprehend them.

The case of Nannie Doss offers valuable insights into the psychological makeup of serial killers, particularly those who operate in domestic settings. Her lack of remorse, cheerful demeanour, and ability to rationalise her actions suggest traits commonly associated with psychopathy and narcissism.

Nannie's crimes were often motivated by self-interest, whether financial or emotional. Her willingness to eliminate anyone who stood in her way, combined with her belief that she was justified in doing so, points to a narcissistic personality. She saw her victims not as individuals with their own needs and desires but as obstacles to be removed.

Nannie's ability to manipulate those around her was central to her success as a killer. She exploited societal norms, familial trust, and her victims' vulnerabilities to achieve her goals. This manipulation extended to her interactions with law enforcement, as her cheerful and cooperative demeanour initially obscured the extent of her crimes.

Nannie Doss's ability to evade detection for so long exposed significant shortcomings in the criminal justice system of her time. Her case revealed how societal biases, inadequate investigative practices, and a lack of interagency communication allowed her to operate with impunity.

One of the most glaring issues in Nannie's case was the failure to conduct autopsies on many of her victims. Had post-mortem examinations been routine, the pattern of arsenic poisoning might have been identified much earlier, potentially saving lives. Her case underscored the importance of treating unexplained deaths with suspicion and ensuring that all potential causes are thoroughly investigated.

Nannie's crimes spanned multiple states, yet there was little communication or coordination between law enforcement agencies. This allowed her to move from one jurisdiction to another without raising red flags. Today, databases like the FBI's Violent Criminal Apprehension Program (ViCAP) help track patterns across jurisdictions, but Nannie's case highlights the ongoing need for collaboration and information sharing.

Nannie Doss's story has had a lasting impact on popular culture, reflecting society's enduring fascination with true crime and the psychology of killers. Her cheerful demeanour, combined with the macabre nature of her crimes, made her a subject of both horror and intrigue.

The media played a significant role in shaping Nannie's legacy, dubbing her "The Giggling Granny" and emphasizing her unsettling combination of charm and cruelty. This coverage contributed to her notoriety, but it also raised ethical questions about how such cases are portrayed. While media attention can help bring awareness to criminal cases, it can also risk sensationalising the perpetrator at the expense of the victims.

Nannie's case is often cited as an example of early public fascination with true crime, a genre that has since grown into a cultural phenomenon. Her story continues to be referenced in books, documentaries, and podcasts, serving as both a cautionary tale and a source of morbid curiosity.

While Nannie Doss's crimes occurred decades ago, the lessons they offer remain relevant today. Her case highlights the importance of vigilance, critical thinking, and systemic improvements in how society handles crime and justice.

Nannie's ability to operate undetected was partly due to her ability to deflect suspicion and exploit trust. Recognising the warning signs of manipulative or predatory behaviour—such as patterns of unexplained deaths or financial exploitation—can help prevent similar cases in the future.

The shortcomings in the investigation of Nannie's crimes underscore the need for continuous improvements in law enforcement practices. Modern tools such as forensic toxicology, DNA analysis, and criminal databases have made it harder for killers like Nannie to evade detection, but her case serves as a reminder that vigilance and thoroughness are essential.

Nannie's case also highlights the dangers of gender biases in criminal investigations. Assumptions about women's capacity for violence allowed her to operate undetected for years, demonstrating the need for impartiality and objectivity in law enforcement.

Deception in the Shadows

Deception has always been an integral part of human behaviour, whether for survival, self-preservation, or malicious intent. However, in the annals of crime, it is often overshadowed by more overt acts of violence and brutality. Yet deception, particularly when it operates in the shadows, has the power to devastate lives in ways that are equally harrowing. Those who weave intricate webs of lies and manipulate others into compliance are often more dangerous than they appear, blending seamlessly into the fabric of society and evading detection for years, sometimes decades.

While high-profile criminals are often at the forefront of public consciousness, it is the lesser-known figures of deception—the unassuming neighbour, the kind colleague, the supportive friend—who remind us of just how vulnerable trust can make us. This chapter delves into the subtle yet insidious art of deception, shedding light on the underexplored cases of manipulative behaviour that operated undetected for years, leaving a legacy of shattered trust and irreparable harm.

The Nature of Deception

Deception is not simply about telling lies; it is a multifaceted act that often involves manipulating reality to serve one's own ends. It can manifest as a carefully constructed false persona, a web of intricate schemes, or the exploitation of trust and vulnerability. Unlike overt acts of aggression, deception operates in the shadows, preying on human instincts to trust and believe in others.

What makes deception particularly dangerous is its reliance on psychological tactics. Manipulative individuals often possess an acute understanding of human behaviour, using charm, empathy, or intimidation to influence their victims. They thrive on the blind spots in human perception, exploiting societal expectations and personal vulnerabilities to gain power and control. While the harm they inflict may not always leave visible scars, its effects are profound and far-reaching, often leaving victims questioning their own judgment and struggling to rebuild their lives.

Why Deceptive Crimes Go Undetected

One of the reasons deceptive crimes often go unnoticed is their subtlety. Unlike violent crimes, which are often immediate and visceral, deception unfolds gradually, giving perpetrators ample time to manipulate their victims and cover their tracks. This slow and calculated approach makes it difficult for victims or bystanders to recognize the harm being done until it is too late.

Societal Blind Spots

Deceptive individuals often exploit societal norms and expectations to avoid suspicion. For example, society tends to view certain roles—parents, spouses, teachers, or caregivers—as inherently trustworthy. Manipulative individuals who occupy these roles can hide in plain sight, using their perceived reliability to deflect scrutiny. Additionally, societal biases, such as the tendency to view women as less capable of malice or older individuals as harmless, can further obscure deceptive behaviour.

Victim Blaming and Shame

Deceptive crimes also go undetected because victims are often reluctant to come forward. Shame, guilt, or fear of being disbelieved can prevent individuals from reporting their experiences. This is particularly true in cases involving financial fraud, emotional manipulation, or betrayal by a trusted individual, where victims may feel complicit or foolish for not recognizing the deception earlier.

The Complexity of Proof

Another challenge in detecting and addressing deceptive crimes is the difficulty of proving them. Deceptive behaviour often involves a lack of tangible evidence, relying instead on patterns of manipulation that can be hard to document or quantify. This creates challenges for law enforcement and judicial systems, which are often more equipped to deal with overt acts of violence than with subtle psychological manipulation.

The Subtle Art of Manipulation

At its core, deception is about power—power over perception, trust, and reality itself. Skilled deceivers understand that their greatest weapon is not physical force but psychological influence. They craft narratives that resonate with their victims, creating a false sense of security that allows them to exploit others without resistance.

Tactics of Deception

Deceptive individuals employ a variety of tactics to achieve their goals, including:

1. **Gaslighting:** Manipulating victims into questioning their own perceptions and memories, making them easier to control.

2. **Feigning Empathy:** Using charm and feigned concern to gain trust and lower the victim's defences.

3. **Exploiting Authority:** Positioning themselves as experts or figures of authority to command obedience or compliance.

4. **Isolating Victims:** Cutting victims off from their support systems to increase their dependency on the manipulator.

5. **Building a False Persona:** Creating a carefully constructed identity that aligns with the victim's needs or expectations.

These tactics are not always overt; they often operate on a subconscious level, leaving victims unaware of the manipulation until it is too late.

The Psychological Impact of Deception

The harm caused by deceptive crimes extends far beyond the immediate loss or betrayal. For many victims, the psychological impact is profound, as the experience undermines their ability to trust others and even themselves. Deception fractures the foundation of human relationships, leaving victims questioning their own judgment and struggling to rebuild their sense of self.

Erosion of Trust

One of the most damaging aspects of deception is the erosion of trust. Victims often feel betrayed not only by the perpetrator but also by their own instincts and perceptions. This can lead to long-term difficulties in forming healthy relationships, as victims may struggle to trust others or fear being manipulated again.

Emotional Trauma

Deceptive crimes often leave victims with deep emotional scars. Feelings of shame, guilt, and self-blame are common, particularly in cases where the deception was prolonged or involved a close relationship. Victims may also experience symptoms of anxiety, depression, and post-traumatic stress disorder as they grapple with the fallout of the manipulation.

Financial and Social Consequences

In cases of financial fraud or professional deception, the consequences can extend beyond the individual victim to their families, businesses, or communities. Financial losses, damaged reputations, and social isolation are common outcomes, further compounding the harm caused by the deception.

Why These Stories Matter

The stories of lesser-known deceivers may not always grab headlines, but they are no less important than those of more infamous criminals. By studying these cases, we gain a deeper understanding of the mechanics of manipulation and the vulnerabilities that make deception possible. These insights are crucial for developing strategies to protect individuals and communities from similar crimes in the future.

Raising Awareness

One of the most important lessons from these cases is the need for greater public awareness of deceptive behaviour. Understanding the tactics and warning signs of manipulation can empower individuals to protect themselves and their loved ones. Education and awareness campaigns can play a crucial role in preventing deceptive crimes and supporting victims.

Improving Investigative Practices

The subtlety of deceptive crimes poses unique challenges for law enforcement and judicial systems. By examining these cases, we can identify areas where investigative practices need to evolve, such as improving the detection of psychological manipulation or developing better tools for tracking financial fraud.

Shifting Societal Norms

Finally, these stories challenge societal norms and assumptions about trust, relationships, and authority. By questioning these norms, we can create a more vigilant and resilient society that is less susceptible to manipulation and exploitation.

The Manipulative Spouse: Love as a Weapon

Marriage, often viewed as a bond built on trust, love, and partnership, represents one of the most intimate relationships in human life. Spouses share financial, emotional, and physical vulnerability with one another, creating an unparalleled level of trust. However, this profound closeness also makes marriage a fertile ground for deception when one partner exploits the relationship for manipulation, control, or personal gain. When love is wielded as a weapon, the consequences can be catastrophic, leaving scars not only on the individuals involved but also on their families and communities.

This chapter delves into the disturbing world of manipulative spouses who weaponised love and trust to harm their partners. From financial exploitation and emotional manipulation to orchestrating murders while maintaining a facade of affection, these stories expose the darker side of marital relationships. Through these cases, we examine the key themes of trust, emotional exploitation, and financial motives, shedding light on how the sacred bonds of marriage can become a stage for betrayal.

Trust as a Tool for Exploitation

Trust is the cornerstone of any marriage, and it is this foundational element that manipulative spouses exploit to achieve their goals. By presenting themselves as loving, supportive partners, they disarm suspicion and gain access to their spouse's finances, emotions, and vulnerabilities. This trust often blinds victims to red flags, allowing the manipulative partner to operate undetected.

Building a False Facade

In many cases, manipulative spouses craft a carefully constructed facade to appear as the ideal partner. This facade is often based on their victim's desires and insecurities. For example, a victim who fears loneliness may be targeted by a partner who feigns unwavering affection, while a financially successful individual might be manipulated by someone who appears to offer stability and emotional support.

The manipulation typically begins with small, seemingly innocuous acts designed to build trust. Over time, as the victim becomes more reliant on their partner, the manipulative spouse begins to exert greater control, often isolating the victim from friends and family to maintain their influence.

Financial Exploitation in Marriages

One of the most common motives for manipulative spouses is financial gain. Marriage provides unparalleled access to a partner's assets, making it an attractive target for those with greed-driven intentions. Whether through embezzling funds, fraud, or inheritance schemes, financial exploitation within marriage is a devastating betrayal.

Marrying for Money

In cases of financial exploitation, some individuals enter marriages with the sole intention of gaining access to their partner's wealth. These marriages are often marked by calculated moves to gain legal or financial control over the victim's assets. For example, a manipulative spouse may persuade their partner to add them to bank accounts, name them as beneficiaries in life insurance policies, or sign over property rights. Once they secure access to these resources, the manipulative spouse may drain accounts, take out loans in their partner's name, or otherwise deplete their wealth.

Case Example: A Spouse's Inheritance Scheme

One chilling case involved a man who married a wealthy widow with the sole intention of gaining control over her estate. Over the course of their relationship, he persuaded her to amend her will, leaving the majority of her assets to him. Shortly after these changes were made, she died under suspicious circumstances. While the man initially appeared to be a grieving husband, investigators later uncovered evidence that he had orchestrated her death to expedite his financial windfall.

Living a Lavish Life at Another's Expense

Another form of financial manipulation involves using marriage to fund a luxurious lifestyle. In these cases, the manipulative spouse showers their partner with affection and promises of love, only to drain their resources over time. Victims may find themselves burdened with debt, facing foreclosure, or bankrupt as a result of their spouse's unchecked spending habits.

Emotional Manipulation and Control

Emotional manipulation is a hallmark of many abusive relationships, particularly those involving manipulative spouses. By exploiting their partner's emotions, insecurities, and fears, these individuals exert control and dominance, often leaving their victims feeling powerless and dependent.

Gaslighting and Psychological Abuse

One of the most insidious forms of emotional manipulation is gaslighting, in which the manipulative spouse undermines their partner's perception of reality. By denying events, twisting facts, or attributing blame to the victim, the manipulative spouse erodes their partner's confidence and self-trust. Over time, this psychological abuse leaves the victim questioning their own judgment and increasingly reliant on the manipulator for validation and guidance.

Isolation as a Tactic

Manipulative spouses often seek to isolate their partners from friends, family, and support networks. This isolation serves two purposes: it increases the victim's dependency on the manipulator and reduces the likelihood of interference from others who might recognize the abuse. Tactics may include sabotaging relationships, controlling communication, or fabricating conflicts to alienate the victim from their loved ones.

Case Example: The Controlling Husband

A particularly harrowing case involved a man who systematically isolated his wife from her family and friends under the guise of protecting her. He convinced her that her loved ones were toxic influences, cutting off all lines of communication. Over time, he gained complete control over her finances, social life, and even her career. By the time she recognized the extent of his manipulation, she had lost her independence and struggled to rebuild her life.

Orchestrating Murders: The Ultimate Betrayal

In the most extreme cases, manipulative spouses resort to murder to achieve their goals. These crimes are often premeditated and driven by financial motives, such as life insurance payouts or inheritance, or by the desire to escape the marriage without facing the consequences of divorce.

Maintaining the Facade

What makes these cases particularly chilling is the ability of the manipulative spouse to maintain the facade of a loving relationship even as they plot their partner's death. In many instances, they continue to act as caring and attentive partners, ensuring that no one suspects their true intentions.

Case Example: The Black Widow

One notorious case involved a woman who married multiple men, each of whom died under mysterious circumstances shortly after their nuptials. Investigators eventually discovered that she had poisoned her husbands to collect life insurance payouts. Throughout each marriage, she had portrayed herself as a devoted wife, carefully hiding her true intentions behind a mask of affection.

Contract Killings

In some cases, manipulative spouses enlist the help of others to carry out their crimes. Hiring a hitman or coercing an accomplice allows them to distance themselves from the act of murder, making it more difficult to trace the crime back to them. These cases often involve elaborate schemes to create alibis and divert suspicion, underscoring the calculated nature of their actions.

Long-Term Betrayal: The Hidden Costs

The impact of a manipulative spouse's actions extends far beyond the immediate harm inflicted on their partner. For victims, the betrayal often leaves lasting emotional, financial, and psychological scars. Rebuilding trust, recovering from financial losses, and processing the trauma of emotional abuse or physical harm can take years, if not a lifetime.

The Ripple Effect

The consequences of these betrayals are rarely confined to the immediate victim. Family members, friends, and even entire communities can be affected. Children, in particular, may suffer long-term emotional and psychological harm as a result of witnessing manipulation, abuse, or betrayal within their parents' marriage.

Challenges in Seeking Justice

For many victims, seeking justice against a manipulative spouse can be an uphill battle. Proving emotional manipulation or financial exploitation often requires extensive evidence, which can be difficult to gather in the context of an intimate relationship. In cases involving murder, the manipulative spouse's ability to conceal their true intentions can complicate investigations and delay accountability.

Lessons from Manipulative Spouses

The stories of manipulative spouses reveal critical lessons about trust, vigilance, and the complexities of human relationships. By understanding the tactics and motives of these individuals, we can better protect ourselves and others from falling victim to similar betrayals.

Recognizing Red Flags

One of the most important takeaways from these cases is the importance of recognizing red flags in a relationship. Signs of manipulation, such as controlling behaviour, gaslighting, or financial secrecy, should not be ignored. Early intervention can prevent these patterns from escalating into more serious harm.

The Importance of Support Networks

Maintaining strong connections with friends, family, and support networks is crucial for recognizing and addressing manipulative behaviour. Isolation is a common tactic used by manipulative spouses, and having external perspectives can help victims identify and resist their partner's influence.

Strengthening Legal Protections

Finally, these cases underscore the need for stronger legal protections for victims of manipulation and abuse. Laws addressing financial exploitation, psychological abuse, and coercive control can provide victims with the tools they need to seek justice and rebuild their lives.

The Fraudulent Friend: Betrayal in Close Circles

Friendship, built on trust, mutual respect, and shared experiences, is one of the most cherished human relationships. Unlike familial or romantic bonds, friendships are often formed by choice, creating a unique space where people feel safe, valued, and understood. However, this trust can also make individuals vulnerable to exploitation. When a friend weaponises that bond for personal gain—be it financial, social, or even criminal—it becomes a devastating betrayal that often leaves emotional and psychological scars far deeper than those inflicted by strangers.

This chapter explores the phenomenon of fraudulent friendships, examining cases where individuals exploited platonic relationships for personal benefit. From financial scams and social manipulation to using friends as unwitting accomplices, these stories highlight the darker side of trust and the devastating impact of betrayal. By understanding the tactics used by deceptive friends and the vulnerabilities they exploit, we can learn to protect ourselves from falling victim to such betrayals.

The Foundation of Trust in Friendships

Friendships are rooted in trust, often involving the sharing of personal stories, secrets, and vulnerabilities. Unlike formal relationships, friendships are voluntary, which makes the trust within them feel more genuine and unforced. This trust is what allows friendships to thrive but also what makes betrayal so painful. When a friend manipulates or exploits the relationship, it shakes the very foundation of trust, leaving the victim feeling isolated and disoriented.

Why We Trust Friends

Friendship is often seen as a sanctuary from the complexities of life. Friends are chosen based on shared values, interests, and emotional connections, creating a sense of safety and comfort. This trust is reinforced through consistent interaction and positive reinforcement, which builds a sense of reliability. Unfortunately, this same trust can blind individuals to the red flags of manipulative or deceitful behaviour.

Deception in Platonic Relationships

Deceptive friends use the trust inherent in friendships to manipulate their victims. Unlike strangers, who must first gain access to their target, a friend already has the victim's confidence and often intimate knowledge of their weaknesses and insecurities. This gives the fraudulent friend a significant advantage, allowing them to exploit the relationship for personal gain.

Forms of Deception

1. **Financial Exploitation:** Borrowing money with no intention of repayment, convincing friends to invest in fraudulent schemes, or outright theft.

2. **Social Manipulation:** Using friendships to gain social status, access to exclusive opportunities, or as a means of controlling the victim's social network.

3. **Emotional Exploitation:** Taking advantage of a friend's vulnerability or loyalty to extract favours, resources, or emotional labour.

4. **Criminal Involvement:** Involving friends in illegal activities, either by coercion or deception, and leaving them to face the consequences.

Financial Betrayal Among Friends

Financial exploitation is one of the most common forms of betrayal in friendships. A deceptive friend may borrow money under false pretences, pressure their victim into investing in a fraudulent scheme, or take advantage of the victim's generosity.

The "Borrow and Forget" Tactic

A fraudulent friend often begins their financial exploitation by asking for small loans, citing personal emergencies or temporary hardships. These loans are typically framed as one-time requests, and the victim, wanting to help their friend, agrees. Over time, the requests may increase in frequency and amount, with the fraudulent friend offering excuses for why they cannot repay. By the time the victim realises what is happening, they may have lost significant sums of money.

Case Example: The Scheming Borrower

In one notable case, a man convinced his close friend to lend him money over the course of several years, claiming he was facing mounting medical bills. The victim, sympathetic to his friend's plight, continued to provide financial support, even dipping into his savings. It was later revealed that the fraudulent friend had no medical issues and had used the money to fund a lavish lifestyle. The betrayal not only left the victim financially devastated but also emotionally broken, struggling to trust anyone again.

Investment Scams Among Friends

Another form of financial betrayal involves persuading friends to invest in fraudulent ventures. These schemes often rely on the victim's trust and the manipulator's ability to create a facade of legitimacy. By the time the victim realises the investment is a scam, the fraudulent friend has vanished or is unwilling to return the funds.

Case Example: The Ponzi Scheme Friend

A woman persuaded several friends to invest in a real estate project, promising high returns. Her charm and apparent expertise made her seem credible, and her friends eagerly handed over their savings. The project, however, was a sham, and the woman used the money to fund her personal expenses. When the scheme collapsed, her friends were left with nothing but shattered trust and financial ruin.

Social Manipulation: Using Friends as Leverage

Beyond financial exploitation, some fraudulent friends manipulate relationships to gain social leverage. These individuals use friendships as tools to climb social ladders, gain access to exclusive opportunities, or manipulate others into fulfilling their personal ambitions.

The Status Seeker

In many cases, a fraudulent friend aligns themselves with someone of higher social status to elevate their own position. They may ingratiate themselves into social circles, using the friendship as a stepping stone while offering little in return. Once they achieve their goal, they often abandon the victim, leaving them feeling used and betrayed.

Case Example: Climbing the Social Ladder

A man befriended a well-connected colleague, using their friendship to secure invitations to exclusive events and introductions to influential people. Over time, he distanced himself from his colleague, focusing instead on maintaining the connections he had gained through the friendship. The colleague, realising he had been used, was left feeling betrayed and isolated.

Manipulating Social Networks

Some fraudulent friends use manipulation to control their victim's social network. They may spread rumours, create divisions, or isolate the victim from other friends and family. This not only increases the victim's dependency on the manipulative friend but also allows the fraudster to maintain control over the situation.

Case Example: The Saboteur

A woman manipulated her friend's social circle by spreading false rumours about mutual acquaintances, causing conflicts and isolating her friend from others. By positioning herself as the victim's only trusted confidant, she gained emotional control and access to the victim's resources.

Emotional Exploitation and Dependency

Emotional exploitation is a particularly insidious form of betrayal, as it often leaves victims questioning their own judgment. Fraudulent friends may exploit their victim's empathy, loyalty, or insecurities to extract emotional labour, favours, or support.

The Perpetual Victim

A common tactic among fraudulent friends is to present themselves as perpetual victims. By sharing exaggerated or fabricated stories of hardship, they evoke sympathy and ensure their victim feels obligated to help. Over time, this dynamic creates an imbalance in the friendship, with the victim consistently giving more than they receive.

Case Example: The Friend in Crisis

A man frequently called upon his best friend for emotional support, claiming to be struggling with various personal crises. The friend devoted significant time and energy to helping him, only to discover that many of the crises were fabricated to gain attention and manipulate the friendship.

Unwitting Accomplices: Friends Drawn into Crime

In some cases, fraudulent friends use deception to involve their victims in criminal activities, often without their knowledge. These scenarios can have devastating consequences, as the victim may face legal repercussions or social ostracism for actions they did not fully understand.

The Unknowing Partner

A manipulative friend may persuade their victim to participate in seemingly innocuous activities that are actually part of a larger criminal scheme. By the time the victim realises the truth, they may be complicit in crimes they did not intend to commit.

Case Example: The Smuggling Scheme

A woman convinced her friend to transport packages across state lines, claiming they contained business documents. In reality, the packages contained illegal substances. When authorities intercepted the shipments, the friend faced criminal charges, while the manipulative woman disappeared without taking responsibility.

The Impact of Betrayal

The betrayal of a friend leaves deep emotional and psychological scars. Victims often struggle to reconcile the trust they once placed in the fraudulent friend with the reality of their actions. This can lead to feelings of shame, self-blame, and difficulty trusting others in the future.

Rebuilding Trust

For many victims, recovering from a fraudulent friendship involves rebuilding their ability to trust. This process can be long and challenging, as the betrayal often shakes their confidence in their own judgment and their ability to discern genuine relationships.

Seeking Justice

In cases of financial exploitation or criminal involvement, victims may pursue legal action against their fraudulent friend. However, proving deception in the context of a friendship can be challenging, as the relationship often lacks formal agreements or documentation.

Lessons from Fraudulent Friendships

The stories of fraudulent friends highlight the importance of vigilance and self-awareness in relationships. While trust is an essential component of friendship, it is important to recognize red flags and maintain healthy boundaries.

Recognizing Manipulative Behaviour

Common warning signs of a fraudulent friend include:

- Frequent requests for money or favours without reciprocation.
- Attempts to isolate the victim from other friends or family.
- Exaggerated or fabricated stories designed to evoke sympathy.
- A lack of accountability or transparency in their actions.

Maintaining Boundaries

Establishing clear boundaries in friendships can help protect against manipulation. This includes setting limits on financial support, emotional labour, and personal involvement.

The Double Life: Ordinary Faces, Extraordinary Secrets

The concept of a "double life" has long fascinated society, serving as the basis for countless stories, novels, and films. The idea that someone could conceal a hidden identity behind the veneer of normalcy is both chilling and intriguing. In real life, individuals leading double lives often appear to be ordinary citizens—hardworking professionals, devoted family members, or respected members of their communities—while secretly engaging in criminal activities or harbouring dark secrets. Their ability to seamlessly blend into society not only helps them evade detection but also amplifies the sense of betrayal and shock when their true identities are revealed.

This chapter delves into the phenomenon of double lives, exploring how individuals manage to maintain outward appearances while concealing criminal or unethical behaviour. From respected professionals who secretly commit heinous crimes to family-oriented individuals hiding dark secrets, these stories reveal the complexities of duality, the power of deception, and the devastating impact on those around them.

The Nature of a Double Life

A double life involves more than just hiding certain behaviours; it requires the individual to create and maintain a façade of normalcy, often going to great lengths to ensure their secret life remains undiscovered. This duality is not merely a strategy for evading detection—it is a skilful manipulation of trust, perception, and societal expectations.

Why People Lead Double Lives

Several factors drive individuals to lead double lives, including:

1. **Desire for Power or Control:** The act of deceiving others and living undetected often gives individuals a sense of superiority or power over those around them.

2. **Financial Gain:** Many double lives are rooted in financial motivations, such as fraud, embezzlement, or illegal schemes.

3. **Fear of Judgment or Consequences:** People who engage in behaviours considered socially unacceptable or criminal may create a false persona to protect themselves from societal judgment or legal repercussions.

4. **Thrill-Seeking:** For some, the danger and excitement of maintaining a double life become addictive, driving them to continue their deception.

The Challenges of Duality

Maintaining a double life requires meticulous planning, as individuals must manage two separate identities without allowing them to overlap. This often involves crafting alibis, hiding physical evidence, and manipulating those around them to deflect suspicion. The constant effort to keep these two worlds separate can lead to immense psychological strain, yet many manage to maintain their deception for years, even decades.

The Hidden Criminal: Ordinary Lives, Extraordinary Crimes

Some of the most shocking examples of double lives involve individuals who appear to be model citizens while secretly engaging in criminal behaviour. These individuals often use their respectable reputations as a shield, making it difficult for others to believe they could be involved in illegal activities.

The Trusted Professional

Professionals in positions of authority or trust, such as doctors, teachers, or clergy, are particularly effective at leading double lives. Their roles grant them a degree of credibility that makes their actions less likely to be questioned.

Case Example: The Charitable Doctor

A highly respected physician who dedicated his free time to charity work was later discovered to be running a prescription drug ring. While he was publicly lauded for his contributions to the community, he used his medical practice to illegally distribute controlled substances, profiting from the addiction crisis. His double life allowed him to operate undetected for years, as his charitable work and professional standing deflected suspicion.

The Family-Oriented Criminal

Another common archetype is the devoted family person who conceals illegal activities behind the appearance of a stable home life. These individuals often leverage their roles as spouses or parents to create an image of reliability and trustworthiness.

Case Example: The Stay-at-Home Father

A stay-at-home father, known for his involvement in local school events and community activities, was later revealed to be running an elaborate counterfeit money operation from his basement. His dedication to his family and community helped him evade detection, as no one suspected that such a seemingly devoted individual could be involved in a federal crime.

Dual Lives in the Workplace

The workplace is another common setting where individuals maintain double lives. Employees in positions of power or access can use their roles to facilitate criminal activities, often exploiting their colleagues' trust and the organization's resources.

Embezzlement and Fraud

Financial crimes, such as embezzlement and fraud, are common among individuals leading double lives in the workplace. These individuals often hold trusted positions, such as accountants, managers, or executives, giving them access to funds or resources they can exploit.

Case Example: The Corporate Fraudster

A high-ranking executive at a multinational company was discovered to have embezzled millions of dollars over a decade. Known for his impeccable work ethic and charm, he gained the trust of his colleagues and superiors, allowing him to siphon funds unnoticed. He maintained his double life by using the stolen money to fund a luxurious lifestyle that he carefully concealed from his professional circle.

Espionage and Insider Threats

In some cases, individuals use their positions in the workplace to engage in espionage or sabotage. These actions often involve selling sensitive information, leaking confidential data, or undermining their employer for personal or ideological reasons.

Case Example: The Undercover Mole

A government contractor with access to classified information was revealed to have been selling secrets to a foreign entity for years. He maintained his cover by excelling in his job, earning accolades for his work while secretly compromising national security.

The Psychological Toll of Living a Lie

Living a double life is not without consequences. The constant need to maintain separate identities often leads to significant psychological stress, including anxiety, paranoia, and emotional exhaustion. Despite these challenges, many individuals continue their deception, either because they fear the consequences of being exposed or because they have become addicted to the thrill of their double life.

Cognitive Dissonance

One of the key psychological challenges faced by individuals leading double lives is cognitive dissonance—the mental discomfort caused by holding conflicting beliefs or behaviours. Balancing two opposing identities requires them to compartmentalize their actions, which can lead to feelings of guilt, shame, or self-loathing.

The Fear of Exposure

The constant fear of being exposed can also take a toll on an individual's mental health. Many live with the anxiety that one mistake—a misplaced document, an overheard conversation, or an unplanned encounter—could unravel their carefully constructed facade. This fear often leads to hypervigilance, secrecy, and isolation, further straining their relationships and emotional well-being.

The Impact on Communities and Relationships

The revelation of a double life often leaves a trail of devastation in its wake, affecting not only the perpetrator but also their family, friends, colleagues, and community. The betrayal of trust can have long-lasting emotional and social consequences for those who believed in the individual's false persona.

The Shock of Betrayal

For those close to the individual, discovering the truth can be deeply traumatic. Family members may feel humiliated or betrayed, while colleagues may struggle to reconcile their perception of the individual with the reality of their actions. This betrayal often leads to feelings of anger, confusion, and mistrust, making it difficult for the victims to move forward.

The Erosion of Trust

The impact of a double life extends beyond personal relationships, eroding trust within communities and organizations. When someone in a position of authority or respect is revealed to have been living a lie, it undermines confidence in similar roles, creating a ripple effect of suspicion and skepticism.

Lessons from Lives of Deception

The stories of individuals leading double lives offer valuable lessons about trust, vigilance, and the complexities of human behaviour. By understanding the tactics used by these individuals and the vulnerabilities they exploit, we can better protect ourselves and our communities.

Recognizing Red Flags

While individuals leading double lives are often skilled at concealing their actions, certain red flags may indicate deception. These include inconsistent behaviour, unexplained absences, or secrecy about personal or professional activities. Learning to recognize these signs can help identify potential double lives before they cause harm.

The Importance of Transparency

Promoting transparency in relationships, workplaces, and communities can help reduce the likelihood of deception. Open communication, accountability, and checks and balances create an environment where individuals are less able to conceal harmful behaviour.

Building Resilience

Finally, the impact of a double life underscores the importance of building resilience in the face of betrayal. By fostering strong support networks and focusing on rebuilding trust, individuals and communities can recover from the shock of deception and move forward with greater awareness and strength.

Conclusion

The stories of individuals leading double lives remind us that appearances can be deceiving and that the most dangerous secrets are often hidden in plain sight. These tales of duality and deception expose the vulnerabilities in human relationships, institutions, and society at large, offering valuable insights into the power of trust and the devastating consequences of betrayal. While the revelation of a double life can leave lasting scars, it also serves as a stark reminder of the importance of vigilance, transparency, and resilience in navigating the complexities of human behaviour.

Professional Deceivers: Con Artists and Fraudsters

In the intricate world of financial deception, the con artist stands as a master manipulator, weaving webs of lies and illusions to achieve one central goal: profit. Unlike violent criminals, con artists rely on charm, persuasion, and meticulous planning to defraud their victims, often targeting businesses, investors, and individuals who trust them implicitly. Their crimes can span years, even decades, leaving behind trails of financial ruin and emotional devastation. Whether orchestrating Ponzi schemes, running long cons, or engaging in elaborate financial frauds, professional deceivers represent a unique class of criminals whose actions exploit society's trust and vulnerabilities.

This chapter delves into the world of professional deceivers, exploring the psychology behind their actions, notable cases of financial schemes, and the broader societal implications of their crimes. By examining the tactics and motivations of con artists, we can better understand the devastating consequences of financial deception and the lessons it offers for prevention and accountability.

The Psychology of a Con Artist

Con artists are skilled manipulators who rely on their ability to influence and deceive others. Their success often stems from a deep understanding of human behaviour, which they use to exploit their victims' emotions, biases, and desires. At the heart of their schemes is the art of persuasion, as they convince others to part with their money or assets under false pretences.

Key Traits of Con Artists

1. **Charm and Charisma:**
Con artists are often exceptionally charismatic, using their charm to build trust and credibility. They present themselves as confident,

trustworthy, and likable, making it difficult for victims to suspect their intentions.

   2. **Manipulative Skills:**

These individuals are adept at identifying their victims' vulnerabilities and tailoring their approach accordingly. Whether it's appealing to greed, fear, or a desire for security, con artists know how to push the right emotional buttons.

   3. **Attention to Detail:**

Professional deceivers meticulously plan their schemes, creating elaborate backstories, forged documents, and convincing narratives to support their deception. This attention to detail allows them to maintain their facade and avoid detection.

   4. **Lack of Empathy:**

A hallmark of con artists is their ability to exploit others without remorse. They view their victims as means to an end, prioritizing their own gain over the financial and emotional well-being of others.

The Long Con: Building Trust Over Time

One of the most effective tools in a con artist's arsenal is the **long con**, a scheme that unfolds over an extended period, allowing the deceiver to build trust and credibility with their victims before executing the fraud. Long cons often involve intricate setups, multiple players, and significant preparation, making them both difficult to detect and devastating in their impact.

Case Example: The Fake Investment Opportunity

A man posing as a successful entrepreneur convinced dozens of investors to fund his startup, promising substantial returns. Over the course of several years, he built a reputation as a savvy businessman, hosting lavish events and showcasing fake financial statements. When the company finally collapsed, it was revealed that the startup had never existed, and he had pocketed millions of dollars in investor funds. The victims, many of whom had considered him a friend, were left financially devastated.

Ponzi Schemes: The Illusion of Success

Perhaps the most infamous type of financial deception is the **Ponzi scheme**, named after Charles Ponzi, who orchestrated one of the first high-profile cases in the early 20th century. Ponzi schemes involve paying returns to earlier investors using the capital from new investors, creating the illusion of a profitable venture. These schemes rely on a constant influx of new money to sustain the operation, ultimately collapsing when the pool of new investors dries up.

The Mechanics of a Ponzi Scheme

1. **Attracting Investors:**
The con artist promotes a seemingly lucrative investment opportunity, often promising high and consistent returns with little risk.

2. **Paying Early Returns:**
Initial investors receive payouts funded by new investors, creating the illusion of legitimacy and attracting more participants.

3. **Collapse:**
As the scheme grows, it becomes increasingly difficult to sustain, eventually leading to its inevitable collapse and the exposure of the fraud.

Case Example: Bernie Madoff

One of the most notorious Ponzi schemes in history was orchestrated by Bernie Madoff, a financier who defrauded thousands of investors out of billions of dollars. For decades, Madoff maintained the appearance of a highly successful money manager, using his reputation and connections to attract wealthy clients. His scheme collapsed in 2008 during the global financial crisis, exposing the full extent of his deception. The case highlighted the dangers of blind trust and the importance of due diligence in financial investments.

Financial Fraud in Professional Settings

Con artists often exploit their positions within businesses or professional networks to commit financial fraud. These crimes can range from embezzlement and insider trading to forging documents and falsifying financial statements. By leveraging their professional roles, fraudsters gain access to resources and networks that enable them to execute their schemes on a larger scale.

The Trusted Accountant

A common scenario involves accountants or financial managers who embezzle funds from their employers or clients. By manipulating financial records and exploiting their access to sensitive information, these individuals can siphon money over long periods without detection.

Case Example: The Embezzling CFO

A chief financial officer of a medium-sized company was discovered to have stolen millions of dollars over a decade by creating fake vendor accounts and redirecting payments to his personal accounts. His position of authority allowed him to avoid scrutiny, as his colleagues trusted him implicitly. The fraud came to light only after an external audit uncovered discrepancies in the company's financial records.

The Role of Societal Trust in Financial Schemes

One of the key factors enabling con artists to succeed is society's reliance on trust. Financial systems, professional networks, and business relationships all depend on a baseline assumption of honesty and integrity. Con artists exploit this trust, using their victims' confidence in institutions or social norms to further their schemes.

Exploiting Institutional Trust

Many financial frauds succeed because victims believe in the legitimacy of the institutions or credentials associated with the con artist. A fraudster posing as a licensed professional, for example, can leverage the trust inherent in that title to deceive others.

Case Example: The Fake Financial Advisor

A man posed as a licensed financial advisor, convincing retirees to entrust him with their life savings. Using forged certifications and a polished demeanour, he created the illusion of credibility, ultimately stealing millions of dollars. The victims, many of whom lost their entire savings, were left to rebuild their lives in the aftermath.

The Social Capital of Charm

Con artists also exploit social capital, using their charm and interpersonal skills to gain access to influential circles or high-net-worth individuals. This social manipulation allows them to cast a wider net, drawing in victims who are reassured by the fraudster's connections or endorsements.

The Devastating Impact of Financial Deception

The consequences of financial fraud extend far beyond monetary loss. For many victims, the betrayal of trust and the emotional toll of being deceived are equally, if not more, damaging. The ripple effects of these crimes can devastate families, businesses, and communities.

Emotional and Psychological Impact
Victims of financial fraud often experience feelings of shame, guilt, and self-blame, questioning how they could have been deceived. This emotional distress can lead to anxiety, depression, and even physical health issues, particularly for those who lose their life savings or retirement funds.

The Broader Economic Impact

Large-scale financial schemes, such as Ponzi schemes or corporate fraud, can have significant economic repercussions. Businesses may collapse, employees lose jobs, and investors face substantial losses, creating ripple effects throughout the economy.

Lessons from Professional Deceivers

The stories of professional deceivers offer valuable lessons about the importance of vigilance, accountability, and skepticism in financial and professional settings. By understanding the tactics used by con artists, individuals and organizations can better protect themselves from falling victim to fraud.

Conducting Due Diligence

One of the most effective ways to prevent financial deception is through due diligence. Verifying credentials, researching investment opportunities, and seeking independent advice can help individuals identify potential scams before they suffer losses.

Promoting Transparency

Transparency and accountability are essential in professional and financial environments. Regular audits, clear documentation, and open communication can reduce the likelihood of fraud and make it easier to detect wrongdoing.

Educating the Public

Raising awareness about common tactics used by con artists can empower individuals to recognize red flags and protect themselves from deception. Public education campaigns, workshops, and online resources are valuable tools in this effort.

Psychological Manipulators: Cult Leaders and Charismatic Liars

Charismatic manipulators and cult leaders represent some of the most disturbing examples of psychological deception, wielding immense influence over large groups of people. Unlike one-on-one deception, which relies on direct personal manipulation, these individuals use their charm, intellect, and carefully crafted personas to control and exploit entire communities. Cult leaders and other charismatic liars achieve their goals through psychological manipulation, exploiting human vulnerabilities, such as the need for belonging, purpose, or security. The consequences of their actions can be devastating, leading to emotional, financial, and even physical harm for their followers.

This chapter delves into the psychology of cult leaders and charismatic manipulators, examining their tactics, their ability to inspire blind loyalty, and the dynamics of groupthink that enable them to maintain control. Through case examples and an exploration of their methods, we uncover the dark power of deception on a collective scale.

The Psychology of Charismatic Manipulation

Cult leaders and charismatic liars rely on their ability to influence the thoughts, emotions, and behaviours of others. At the core of their success is their ability to create a sense of connection and trust, even when their motives are deeply self-serving. Their power lies not in physical force but in psychological control, which they achieve through a combination of persuasion, coercion, and deception.

Key Traits of Charismatic Manipulators

1. **Charisma and Persuasiveness:**
These individuals possess an uncanny ability to captivate others with their words, body language, and presence. They are often articulate,

confident, and skilled at presenting themselves as trustworthy or enlightened.

2. **Emotional Intelligence:**
Charismatic manipulators are adept at reading the emotions and vulnerabilities of others, using this insight to tailor their approach to each individual or group.

3. **Grandiosity:**
Cult leaders often portray themselves as extraordinary figures, claiming unique knowledge, divine authority, or special abilities that set them apart from ordinary people.

4. **Lack of Empathy:**
Like many other deceivers, charismatic manipulators often lack empathy, viewing their followers as tools to be used for their own gain rather than as individuals with their own needs and desires.

The Tactics of Cult Leaders

The success of cult leaders and psychological manipulators lies in their ability to exploit universal human needs and desires. They craft narratives that appeal to their followers' sense of purpose, belonging, or fear, creating a psychological dependency that makes it difficult to break free.

1. Creating a Vision of Utopia

Cult leaders often present their followers with an idealized vision of the future, promising salvation, enlightenment, or freedom from societal oppression. This vision serves as a powerful motivator, encouraging individuals to abandon their previous lives and dedicate themselves to the cause.

Case Example: A Vision of Salvation

One cult leader claimed to have received divine revelations about the end of the world. He convinced his followers that only those who joined his group and adhered to his teachings would be spared from the impending apocalypse. His apocalyptic narrative created a sense of urgency, leading followers to sell their possessions and sever ties with their families in preparation for the end times.

2. Isolating Followers from Outside Influence

Isolation is a key tactic used by cult leaders to maintain control over their followers. By cutting them off from friends, family, and outside perspectives, they create an echo chamber where their authority goes unchallenged.

How Isolation Works

- Followers are encouraged to distance themselves from "non-believers" or critics who might challenge the leader's teachings.
- Physical isolation, such as living in a communal compound, reinforces dependence on the group.
- Leaders often frame the outside world as corrupt or dangerous, fostering a sense of "us versus them."

3. Instilling Fear and Guilt

Cult leaders frequently use fear and guilt to control their followers. By instilling a fear of punishment—whether spiritual, emotional, or physical—they ensure compliance and discourage dissent. Similarly, guilt is used to manipulate followers into believing they are indebted to the leader or the group.

Case Example: Fear of Divine Retribution

A self-proclaimed prophet convinced his followers that any deviation from his teachings would result in eternal damnation. This fear of divine punishment kept followers in line, even when they were asked to perform extreme or unethical acts in his name.

4. Establishing a Hierarchy

Cult leaders often position themselves at the top of a rigid hierarchy, demanding absolute loyalty and obedience from their followers. By presenting themselves as infallible or divinely chosen, they suppress dissent and maintain their authority.

The Role of Enforcers

Many cults include inner circles or enforcers who help the leader maintain control. These individuals often act as intermediaries, carrying out the leader's orders and ensuring that followers remain compliant.

5. Manipulating Group Dynamics

Groupthink plays a critical role in cult environments. By fostering a sense of unity and shared purpose, cult leaders create an atmosphere where followers are less likely to question the group's actions or beliefs. The fear of ostracism or punishment further discourages dissent.

The Devastating Impact on Followers

The consequences of psychological manipulation by cult leaders are often severe, with followers experiencing financial, emotional, and physical harm. The longer individuals remain under the influence of a manipulative leader, the more difficult it becomes for them to extricate themselves from the situation.

1. Emotional and Psychological Damage

Followers of cults often experience significant emotional and psychological harm, including:

- **Loss of Autonomy:** Followers are stripped of their ability to think critically or make decisions for themselves.
- **Identity Erosion:** Cult leaders often encourage followers to abandon their previous identities, replacing them with new ones defined by the group.
- **Trauma:** Many cults employ tactics of fear, shame, or abuse, leaving lasting scars on their followers.

2. Financial Exploitation

Many cult leaders use their influence to drain their followers' financial resources, convincing them to donate money, sell possessions, or work for free in service of the group.

Case Example: Financial Ruin

A charismatic fraudster posing as a spiritual guru convinced his followers to donate their life savings to fund the construction of a "sacred temple." After collecting millions of dollars, he disappeared, leaving his followers financially destitute and emotionally shattered.

3. Physical Harm

In some cases, the manipulation of cult leaders leads to physical harm or even death. From mass suicides to coerced acts of violence, the consequences of psychological manipulation can be catastrophic.

The Legacy of Charismatic Liars

The stories of cult leaders and charismatic manipulators leave a lasting impact, not only on their victims but also on society at large. These cases highlight the dangers of unchecked power, the vulnerabilities inherent in human nature, and the need for vigilance in the face of deception.

Understanding Vulnerability

By examining the tactics used by cult leaders, we gain insight into the vulnerabilities that make individuals susceptible to manipulation. These include:

- **Desire for Belonging:** Many people join cults because they are searching for connection, purpose, or community.

- **Fear of Uncertainty:** Cult leaders often exploit fears about the future, presenting themselves as sources of stability or guidance.

- **Trust in Authority:** Followers may be inclined to trust leaders who present themselves as experts or enlightened figures.

Lessons for Prevention

Educating individuals about the tactics of psychological manipulation can help prevent future victims from falling prey to cult leaders and charismatic liars. Key strategies include:

- Promoting critical thinking and skepticism.

- Encouraging open communication and support networks.

- Providing resources for those seeking to leave manipulative groups.

Overlooked Justice: Why Deceptive Crimes Are Often Missed

Deceptive crimes are among the most insidious acts of wrongdoing. Unlike overt violence or large-scale scandals, these crimes often slip under the radar, leaving victims in financial, emotional, or psychological ruin before anyone realises a crime has even occurred. Whether orchestrated by manipulative individuals or organised networks, the success of deceptive crimes lies in their ability to blend into the ordinary fabric of life. This makes them notoriously difficult to detect, investigate, and prosecute. From societal blind spots to systemic challenges in law enforcement, the reasons deceptive crimes often go overlooked are as complex as the crimes themselves.

This chapter examines why certain deceptive crimes evade scrutiny, analysing societal biases, systemic gaps, and the subtle nature of these offences. By exploring overlooked justice, we uncover the structural and psychological barriers that allow such crimes to persist undetected for years.

The Subtle Nature of Deceptive Crimes

Deceptive crimes are unique in that they rarely involve the immediate, visceral impact associated with violent or property crimes. Instead, they unfold gradually, often masked by plausible explanations, charm, or elaborate narratives. This subtlety is a key reason why these crimes frequently go unnoticed until significant damage has been done.

Delayed Detection

One of the primary challenges of identifying deceptive crimes is the time it takes for patterns to emerge. For instance, financial fraud often relies on small, repeated actions over a long period, such as embezzlement or Ponzi schemes. By the time a victim realises what has occurred, the perpetrator may have vanished, or the damage may be too extensive to repair.

The Lack of Immediate Harm

Unlike crimes such as theft or assault, which leave immediate, tangible evidence, deceptive crimes often leave behind little more than confusion and financial loss. Victims may not even recognise that they have been deceived, particularly if the perpetrator has carefully constructed a relationship of trust or authority. This delayed awareness complicates investigations and allows perpetrators to continue their schemes unabated.

Societal Blind Spots: Who We Believe and Why

Societal blind spots play a significant role in enabling deceptive crimes. Perpetrators exploit stereotypes, biases, and cultural norms to avoid suspicion, blending seamlessly into their environments and deflecting scrutiny.

The Power of Stereotypes

Society tends to associate certain types of crime with specific demographics, which creates blind spots when perpetrators fall outside these preconceived notions. For instance:

- Women are often perceived as less capable of committing financial or violent crimes, making female con artists or poisoners less likely to be suspected.

- Older individuals, especially those with grandmotherly or grandfatherly demeanours, are typically seen as harmless, which can obscure their involvement in deceptive activities.

- Individuals in positions of authority—such as doctors, clergy, or financial advisors—are often afforded a degree of trust that makes their actions less likely to be questioned.

Case Example: Exploiting Gender Bias

A woman running a long-term fraud operation presented herself as a caring, maternal figure in her community. Her gender and nurturing persona deflected suspicion for years, even as she systematically embezzled funds from local organisations. It was only when her financial discrepancies became impossible to ignore that law enforcement began investigating her activities.

Charisma and Perceived Authority

Charismatic individuals often use their charm and confidence to manipulate perceptions, convincing others of their trustworthiness. This can make victims and even investigators reluctant to believe that such a likable or respectable person could commit a crime.

Case Example: The Trusted Philanthropist

A well-known philanthropist in a small town was later revealed to have defrauded donors by pocketing funds meant for charity. His charm and public generosity had insulated him from suspicion, allowing him to exploit trust for years before being exposed.

Gender Bias in Justice Systems

Gender bias within law enforcement and the judicial system further compounds the issue of overlooked deceptive crimes. Women, in particular, are less likely to be suspected of criminal behaviour, especially in cases involving financial fraud or psychological manipulation.

Assumptions About Gender Roles

Traditional gender roles often paint women as caregivers and nurturers, which can make accusations of deception or exploitation seem implausible. This bias can hinder investigations, as law enforcement may overlook female perpetrators or fail to take victims' claims seriously.

Case Example: The Poisoner

A female caregiver who poisoned her patients to collect life insurance payouts evaded detection for years. Investigators initially attributed the deaths to natural causes, influenced by her role as a nurse and the assumption that she was devoted to her patients' well-being.

Double Standards in Accountability

When women are caught committing deceptive crimes, they may face less severe consequences due to societal perceptions of vulnerability or victimhood. This double standard not only undermines justice but also perpetuates the idea that women are less capable of such crimes, creating further blind spots.

Systemic Challenges in Law Enforcement

Law enforcement agencies face significant obstacles when investigating deceptive crimes. These challenges often stem from resource limitations, gaps in expertise, and the inherently complex nature of such offences.

Resource Allocation

Deceptive crimes often require extensive investigation, including forensic accounting, interviews with multiple victims, and the analysis of years' worth of records. However, many police departments lack the resources or expertise to conduct these in-depth investigations, particularly in smaller jurisdictions where violent crimes take priority.

The Focus on Immediate Threats

Law enforcement agencies are often under pressure to prioritise crimes that pose an immediate threat to public safety, such as violent or drug-related offences. This can result in deceptive crimes being deprioritised, especially if they appear to involve financial disputes or personal grievances rather than clear criminal intent.

Jurisdictional Issues

Many deceptive crimes involve multiple jurisdictions, particularly in cases of financial fraud or cybercrime. The lack of coordination between agencies can hinder investigations, allowing perpetrators to exploit gaps in communication and accountability.

Case Example: The Cross-Border Scammer

An international con artist targeted victims in multiple countries, using fake identities and offshore bank accounts to evade detection. Jurisdictional challenges and delays in information sharing allowed him to continue his schemes for years before being apprehended.

Unspoken Crimes: Why Victims Stay Silent

Victims of deceptive crimes often face significant barriers to reporting their experiences. Shame, fear, and mistrust can prevent individuals from coming forward, allowing perpetrators to continue their activities without consequence.

The Stigma of Being Deceived

Many victims feel embarrassed or ashamed of being deceived, particularly in cases involving financial fraud or emotional manipulation. They may blame themselves for not recognising the signs earlier, fearing judgment from others or further victimisation.

Case Example: The Financial Fraud Victim

A retired couple who lost their life savings to a fraudulent investment scheme chose not to report the crime, fearing public humiliation and the perception that they had been foolish or naive.

Fear of Retaliation

In cases where perpetrators maintain close relationships with their victims, such as friendships or familial ties, victims may fear retaliation or social ostracism if they come forward. This is particularly common in cases of emotional or psychological manipulation, where the victim may already feel isolated or powerless.

Lack of Trust in the System

Some victims hesitate to report deceptive crimes because they believe law enforcement will not take their claims seriously. This lack of trust in the justice system can be especially pronounced in communities with a history of systemic bias or neglect.

Systemic Gaps in Investigation

Beyond resource limitations, systemic gaps in how deceptive crimes are investigated contribute to their underreporting and underprosecution.

Lack of Specialised Training

Many law enforcement agencies lack the specialised training needed to identify and investigate deceptive crimes, particularly those involving complex financial transactions or psychological manipulation. This knowledge gap allows perpetrators to exploit legal and procedural loopholes.

Overreliance on Physical Evidence

Deceptive crimes often leave behind little physical evidence, making them difficult to prove in court. Investigators may dismiss cases that lack tangible proof, even when victims present compelling circumstantial evidence.

Underestimation of Psychological Impact

The psychological toll of deceptive crimes is often underestimated or dismissed, leading to a lack of urgency in addressing these cases. Victims may be seen as overreacting or exaggerating, particularly in cases involving emotional or psychological manipulation.

The Role of Technology in Modern Deception

In the digital age, technology has become both a tool for deceptive crimes and a barrier to justice. Online platforms allow perpetrators to reach a wider audience, conceal their identities, and operate with relative anonymity.

Cybercrime and Fraud

Online scams, such as phishing schemes and fraudulent e-commerce sites, have become increasingly common. These crimes often go unreported or unresolved due to the difficulty of tracking down perpetrators who operate in virtual spaces.

Social Media Manipulation

Social media platforms have created new opportunities for psychological manipulation, as perpetrators can curate false personas and exploit the trust of their followers. These crimes are particularly difficult to detect, as the perpetrators often hide behind layers of anonymity.

Addressing Overlooked Justice

While the challenges of addressing deceptive crimes are significant, there are steps that can be taken to improve detection, investigation, and prosecution.

Education and Awareness

Raising public awareness about the tactics used in deceptive crimes can empower individuals to recognise red flags and protect themselves. Educational campaigns should focus on building critical thinking skills and promoting vigilance in financial and personal interactions.

Strengthening Law Enforcement Resources

Investing in specialised training and resources for law enforcement can improve their ability to investigate deceptive crimes. This includes hiring forensic accountants, psychologists, and cybercrime experts to address the unique challenges posed by these offences.

Encouraging Victim Reporting

Creating safe, supportive environments for victims to report deceptive crimes is essential. This includes reducing the stigma around victimisation, providing resources for emotional support, and ensuring that law enforcement takes all claims seriously.

Lessons from the Shadows: Protecting Against Deception

Deceptive crimes often unfold quietly, with victims realising the truth only after significant harm has been done. These cases, whether involving manipulative individuals, con artists, or seemingly trustworthy figures, highlight the dangers of misplaced trust and the vulnerabilities inherent in human relationships. However, they also offer valuable lessons about how individuals and systems can protect themselves from manipulation and deception. By understanding the tactics of deceivers, recognising red flags, and fostering a culture of vigilance, we can mitigate the impact of such crimes and empower ourselves to navigate a world where appearances can be deceiving.

This chapter explores the lessons learned from lesser-known cases of deception, focusing on strategies for prevention, fostering resilience, and cultivating awareness to protect against manipulative behaviour.

The Nature of Deception

Before delving into specific lessons, it is essential to understand why deception works. Deception relies on exploiting human vulnerabilities—trust, fear, greed, or the desire for connection. Whether through charm, authority, or psychological manipulation, deceivers craft narratives that align with their victims' needs or expectations, making their actions seem credible and their intentions benign.

Universal Vulnerabilities

1. **Trust and Familiarity:**

Most people instinctively trust those they know, particularly friends, family, or individuals in positions of authority. Deceivers exploit this trust by positioning themselves as reliable or familiar figures.

2. **Emotional Needs:**

Emotional vulnerabilities, such as loneliness, fear, or the desire for validation, make individuals more susceptible to manipulation. Deceivers often tailor their approaches to exploit these emotional needs.

3. **Societal Norms:**

Social conventions, such as politeness or respect for authority, can inhibit individuals from questioning suspicious behaviour. Deceivers rely on these norms to avoid scrutiny and maintain their facade.

Understanding these vulnerabilities is the first step toward building defences against deception.

Recognising Red Flags: Early Detection of Deceptive Behaviour

One of the most effective ways to protect against deception is to recognise the warning signs of manipulative behaviour. While every case is unique, certain red flags are common among deceivers and can signal the need for caution.

Inconsistencies in Behaviour or Story

Deceivers often create elaborate narratives to support their schemes. However, maintaining these falsehoods can lead to inconsistencies. Look for contradictions in their stories, unexplained gaps in their history, or behaviour that doesn't align with their claims.

Lesson: Question the Plausible

While it's natural to give people the benefit of the doubt, it's essential to question details that don't add up. Politely asking for clarification or seeking independent verification can help identify potential deception.

Excessive Charm or Flattery

Many deceivers use charm and flattery to disarm suspicion and win trust. While friendliness is not inherently suspicious, excessive or over-the-top behaviour may indicate an ulterior motive.

Lesson: Balance Intuition with Evidence

Relying solely on gut feelings can be dangerous, especially when dealing with charismatic individuals. Balancing intuition with objective evidence can help assess a person's intentions more accurately.

Urgency and Pressure

Deceivers often create a sense of urgency to prevent their victims from thinking critically or seeking advice. This tactic is particularly common in financial scams, where the perpetrator pressures the victim to make immediate decisions.

Lesson: Slow Down

Taking the time to think through decisions, consult trusted advisors, and verify information can prevent impulsive actions that lead to harm.

Building Awareness: Educating Individuals and Communities

Awareness is a powerful tool for combating deception. By educating individuals and communities about the tactics used by deceivers, we can empower people to protect themselves and others.

Public Awareness Campaigns

Governments, non-profits, and media outlets can play a vital role in raising awareness about deceptive practices. Campaigns that highlight common scams, manipulation tactics, and real-life case studies can help individuals recognise and avoid potential threats.

Example: Fraud Prevention Initiatives

Public service announcements about phishing scams, Ponzi schemes, or identity theft have been successful in reducing victimisation. Expanding such initiatives to include lesser-known forms of deception, such as emotional manipulation or workplace fraud, can have a broader impact.

Educational Programs

Incorporating lessons on critical thinking, emotional intelligence, and financial literacy into school curriculums can equip future generations with the skills needed to navigate deception. Workshops for adults, particularly in vulnerable populations such as the elderly, can also be effective.

Lesson: Knowledge is Protection

Educated individuals are less likely to fall victim to deception. By fostering a culture of learning and vigilance, communities can become more resilient to manipulative behaviour.

Strengthening Systems: Prevention at the Institutional Level

While individual vigilance is essential, systemic protections are equally important. Institutions, including businesses, governments, and law enforcement agencies, must address the gaps that allow deception to thrive.

Enhanced Vetting and Background Checks

Many deceptive individuals gain access to their victims through positions of trust or authority. Implementing rigorous vetting processes, including background checks and reference verifications, can help prevent unqualified or malicious individuals from exploiting these roles.

Example: Workplace Fraud Prevention

Companies can reduce the risk of internal fraud by conducting thorough background checks on employees, implementing regular audits, and establishing clear accountability protocols.

Improved Reporting Mechanisms

Encouraging victims to report deceptive behaviour is critical to addressing the problem. Anonymous reporting systems, victim support hotlines, and accessible complaint processes can make it easier for individuals to come forward.

Lesson: Encourage Transparency

Institutions that promote transparency and accountability are less likely to become breeding grounds for deception. Creating a culture where whistleblowers feel safe and supported is key.

Collaboration Across Jurisdictions

Deceptive crimes often span multiple jurisdictions, particularly in cases involving financial fraud or cybercrime. Strengthening collaboration between local, national, and international agencies can improve the detection and prosecution of such crimes.

Resilience in the Face of Deception

Even with the best preventative measures, some level of deception is inevitable. Building resilience—both at the individual and societal level—can mitigate the impact of these crimes and help victims recover.

Emotional Resilience

For victims of deception, the emotional aftermath can be just as devastating as the material loss. Feelings of betrayal, shame, and anger are common, but resilience can help individuals move forward.

Steps to Emotional Recovery

1. **Acknowledge the Experience:**
Accepting that deception has occurred is the first step toward healing. Victims should remind themselves that being deceived is not a reflection of their intelligence or worth.

2. **Seek Support:**
Talking to trusted friends, family, or mental health professionals can provide valuable perspective and emotional validation.

3. **Focus on Growth:**
While the experience of deception is painful, it can also be a learning opportunity. Reflecting on the incident can help individuals identify patterns and strategies to avoid future victimisation.

Community Resilience

At the community level, fostering connections and mutual support can reduce the impact of deception. When individuals feel connected and supported, they are more likely to seek help and share information, creating a collective defence against manipulation.

The Importance of Trust and Vigilance

One of the most challenging aspects of protecting against deception is balancing trust with vigilance. Trust is essential for building meaningful relationships and functioning communities, but blind trust can create opportunities for exploitation.

Healthy Skepticism

Being vigilant does not mean being cynical. Healthy skepticism involves questioning information and motives without assuming malicious intent. This balanced approach allows individuals to protect themselves while maintaining trust in others.

Lesson: Verify Before Trusting

Whether in financial transactions, personal relationships, or professional interactions, verifying information and seeking independent perspectives can prevent many forms of deception.

Building a Culture of Trust

While deception can undermine trust, it is possible to rebuild it through transparency, accountability, and education. By fostering a culture of trust that prioritises honesty and integrity, communities can become more resilient to manipulation.

THE KILLER NEXT DOOR

The Ordinary Faces of Murder

K. ELEANOR